1

Camelot

THE DRAGONS

1
Camelot

Colin Thompson

illustrations by the author

X

RANDOM HOUSE AUSTRALIA

A Random House book
Published by Random House Australia Pty Ltd
Level 3, 100 Pacific Highway, North Sydney NSW 2060
www.randomhouse.com.au

First published by Random House Australia in 2009

Addresses for companies within the Random House Group can be found at www.randomhouse.com.au/offices.

National Library of Australia
Cataloguing-in-Publication Entry

Author: Thompson, Colin (Colin Edward)
Title: Camelot / Colin Thompson
ISBN: 978 1 74166 381 5 (pbk.)
Series: Thompson, Colin (Colin Edward). Dragons; 1
Target audience: For primary school age
Dewey number: A823.3

Design, illustrations and typesetting by Colin Thompson
Printed and bound by The SOS Print + Media Group, Australia

Random House Australia uses papers that are natural, renewable and recyclable products and made from wood grown in sustainable forests. The logging and manufacturing processes are expected to conform to the environmental regulations of the country of origin.

10 9 8 7 6 5 4

For Donald, who is now big enough to have a book of his own.*

Camelot – the home of Kings and Queens and Noble Knights and Magic and lots of Nanas, Fremsley the Royal Whippet, a unique breed of Cockroach, some weird fishy things and aggressive Lavatories.

Long ago in a faraway land, nearly halfway between somewhere over the rainbow and 23 Paradise Street, Arcadia, was a magical land called Avalon.

And at the heart of Avalon was a magical castle called Camelot.

And at the heart of Camelot lived a mighty King called Uther-Pendragon.[1]

Camelot was a fabulous place, so fabulous indeed that it was almost impossible to believe it really existed and wasn't just a wonderful dream.

Even the greatest stories written about it did not do it justice. It was the ultimate castle, more magnificent and vast than the next ten best castles added together. It wasn't just staggeringly gorgeous, it was staggeringly big too. It didn't have one room for each day of the year, it had eleven and a half.

The moat that surrounded the castle wasn't so much a wide strip of water as a vast lake. There were islands in the moat, over three hundred of them,

---

[1]   *I know. It's a ridiculous name, but I didn't make it up. King Arthur's dad was really called that. It's probably Olde Medieval English for Nigel.*

1

each with their own story to tell.[2]

To reach the castle itself you had to cross seven of the islands, which were linked to each other by a narrow stone bridge only wide enough to allow horses to cross them in single file. On the seventh island there was a gatehouse. To cross the final stretch of water the gatehouse keeper would send a carrier pigeon across to the castle with a Request of Access. Once this had been granted – and it was by no means guaranteed that it would be – a team of sixteen enormous horses would walk slowly across the great courtyard in the centre of the castle, feeding out the two great chains that lowered the final link, a drawbridge of ancient timbers that were rumoured to have come from the hull of Noah's Ark itself.

So going to Camelot was not a journey for the faint of heart. Nor was it meant to be. The journey across the moat could take weeks, depending on who it was you wanted to visit, and the mood of the Overseer of Requests of Access, who had a very bad-tempered wife. If his wife, Irongirder, had

[2] *Except islands can't actually talk, apart from the Talking Island, which never stops talking.*

been particularly horrible to him that day, then the Overseer could take ages to process the forms. There were times when the island where the gatehouse stood was so overcrowded that people were falling into the water at a rate of about one per minute. This was something that seldom ended well because of the olms.[3]

In Camelot's moat, the olms grow big enough to swallow a horse, which they often do. The largest and oldest olm, Krakatoa, had lived in the moat since the ancient days, which ended about half an hour before time began. Olms do not eat knights. They just suck off their armour and cover them with slime that is slimier than any slime you have ever seen and smells dreadful. Knights this has happened to are sent to the Downwind Islands at the far end of the moat until the smell wears off, which can take years.[4]

---

[3] *There really is a creature called an olm – look on Google. They are strange, blind creatures which eat, sleep and breed underwater and are also known as 'human fish' because their skin looks like human skin. They usually grow up to 40 centimetres long. They only live in subterranean caves in parts of Southern Europe, and in the moat at Camelot.*

[4] *See page 17 for a tourist brochure about the Downwind Islands, one of the lovely places to holiday around Camelot.*

3

Because it was so difficult to reach, Camelot did not have a lot of visitors. It hadn't always been this way. Originally, the moat had been like every other moat, a narrow strip of deep, murky water full of ferocious crocodiles, mind-numbingly vicious bacteria and tiny snails that crawled into any part of a human body that had a hole in it. This was how all moats were and how most still are to this day. But despite all the life-threatening stuff, there were still people who made it across to the castle. So the King of Avalon at the time, Great-grandfather Pendragon, asked Merlin, the castle's resident wizard, to fix it. That is how the moat became a lake, the tiny snails grew razor-sharp spikes on their shells and the mind-numbingly vicious bacteria evolved into the clerical staff that created all the forms you had to fill out before you could even set foot on the first of the seven islands.

But Camelot was so exquisitely beautiful that, by comparison, even the Blue Bird of Paradise looked as ugly as a bald eighty-seven-year-old hippopotamus with cracked skin and one ear. The castle's reputation spread throughout the land and lots of other places

too. People would travel for days simply to stand on the edge of the moat and admire Camelot's legendary gorgeousness. As they gazed across calm waters where swallows dipped and swans glided majestically by, they would be overwhelmed by a feeling of wonderful tranquility. Unfortunately, the trouble with feelings of wonderful tranquility is that they make people light-headed, and the trouble with being light-headed is that you lose your balance, and the trouble with losing your balance when you are standing on the edge of Camelot's moat is falling in. This is why the olms of Camelot are so huge. They get a lot of food.

The Attic of Nanas, where Old Nannies while away their Twilight Years knitting Awful Cardigans and dribbling down their vests and the vest of anyone else stupid enough to get too close to them.

Rich children have privileges that ordinary kids like you do not. Obviously Arthur, being the son of Uther-Pendragon, King of Avalon, had all sorts of privileges that common people couldn't even dream of. One of these privileges was having a nanny.

Arthur's nanny was called Nana Agnys.

Nannies are a privilege that some people might not see as one. Some people might even think that only seeing your real mother for five minutes at six o'clock every evening except on weekends was a bad thing.

Arthur was not one of those people.

His mother, Queen Igraine[5] – or at least, the lady that Nana Agnys said was Arthur's mother – was a distant, unfeeling woman who smelled of dead roses and rhubarb. Every evening at six o'clock Nana Agnys took young Arthur down to the castle dining hall to see her. And five minutes later she took him back up to the nursery.

Queen Igraine greeted her son with the same expression she might have had if she had just

---

[5] *After whom the awful headache the migraine is named.*

7

discovered she had trodden in something a puppy had left behind. Both mother and son looked forward to five past six with great anticipation. It was actually the only thing that Igraine and Arthur had in common.

These five-minute meetings were the only contact Arthur ever had with his parents. The King didn't even know that Camelot had a nursery, never mind where it was, and the Queen thought the nursery was two old patches of mud by the castle walls where the cook grew beetroots.

'Tell me again, Nana,' Arthur always asked as Nana Agnys led him back upstairs, 'who is that lady?'

'She is your mother,' Nana Agnys always replied, 'and the big hairy man at the other end of the table is your father, the King.'

'And that stuff they were eating that smelled so wonderful?' Arthur asked as he tucked into his nightly bowl of gruel and goat's hoof.

'That is meat, my dear.'

'And those lovely shiny white things the meat was on, Nana, what are they?'

'Plates.'

8

'Gosh. When I am King shall I get meat to eat?'

'Of course, my dear,' Nana Agnys replied. 'When you are King you will be able to eat anything you want.'

'Gosh, and when I am King, shall I eat my meat off a shiny white plate and use the pointy metal things?'

'Knives and forks. Of course you shall,' said Nana Agnys, patting the boy affectionately on his head.

'Gosh, and when I am King, shall I still have to go and see that lady, um, er . . .'

'Your mother.'

'Yes, her. Shall I still have to go and see her every night at six o'clock except weekends?'

'Not if you don't want to, my dear.'

'I shan't want to, thank you,' said Arthur. 'In fact, I think I shall want to banish her to that little castle on the grey island at the far side of the lake that makes your eyes water.'

'You mean . . .?'

'Yes, Nana, I shall banish her to the Island of Onions.'

'I think you mean the Island of Shallot, my treasure,' said Nana Agnys.

'Whatever, Nana,' said Arthur. 'When I am King, I shall rename it the Island of Vegetables, and then there will be no more confusion.'

'Clever boy.'

Arthur licked the last of his gruel from the rough wooden bowl, picked the splinters out of his tongue, picked gravel that had been caught in the goat's hoof out of his teeth, handed the hoof to Nana Agnys to wash ready to add to his gruel the next night, and then said, 'And how shall I become King again, Nana?'

'You shall become King when your father dies,' said Nana Agnys.

'Do you think that might be soon, Nana, for I should so like to eat meat from a plate?'

'No, my child, your father is in fine health.'

'But his hair is grey and he looks terribly old.'

'Only to a child as young as you, my dear. Your father is in his prime and will rule over us for many years to come.'

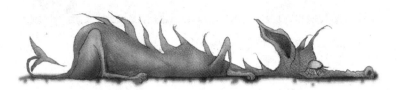

As the nightly-except-weekends five-minute visits to his parents' dinner table mounted up, the intoxicating smell of roast venison and roast pheasant and roast lamb and roast swan sank deeper and deeper into Arthur's brain, until it was with him every waking minute of every day, including weekends.

Then, when Arthur was eleven years old, he was summoned to his parents' table, not at six o'clock in the evening, but at breakfast time on Christmas Day.

This had never happened before and it did not mean that his parents were planning something that normal parents would do, like give him a hug and a nice present. He was summoned because Merlin had suggested to the King that doing so might show the people that he was a good and kind father. The King, although confused, had agreed. There was no hug and no present, just the same flat questions he got every evening. The only difference was that instead of asking him how his day had been, his mother asked

him how his night had been. Then Nana Agnys took him away again.

But there had been one other thing that was different.

Something so powerful that it surpassed everything else. Suddenly the smell of roast venison, pheasant, lamb and swan all sank into second place. Because the air had been filled with a certain kind of magic. Such a powerful magic that it would change the course of history.

Bacon.

The scent of crispy bacon was the final piece of the jigsaw that told Arthur what he must do.

'Daddy must become dead,' he whispered into the darkness, revealing the hint of nastiness that was actually his true nature, but that had been hidden by the fact that he was a blond-haired, sweet-faced eleven-year-old boy who had to eat gruel every night.

Nanas are different from other people. They are a strange race of old ladies who are born old. Not for them the joys and miseries of being a child, growing up, falling in and out of love. They are born exactly as they will be for the rest of their lives. No one knows where they come from, not even the nanas themselves. They are created only to be nanas.

When a rich lady has a baby, she very quickly realises that she simply doesn't have enough time any more to go shopping to buy all the important things she will need for the coming season's round of parties and balls, and get her hair done, and attend coffee mornings every day. When this happens, her husband buys her a nana. These are not to be confused with what poor people refer to as nanas. No, these are not grandmothers. These are proper nanas and only posh rich people can get them. There is a secret phone number for the Nana Shop that rich people are born with, tattooed inside their left nostril.

No number up the nose = no nana.

Those lucky enough to have the number call up and the next morning a brand-new old nana is delivered to their door, instantly relieving them of

13

smelly nappies, sore bottoms, baby spew and endless embarrassing questions about where babies come from.

Apart from those rare children who actually think spending time with their parents is quite nice, everyone is much happier when their nana arrives.

Mummies can do even more shopping, Pilates and being pampered.

Daddies can do, well, actually, daddies can carry on doing exactly the same as they were doing before the little sprog[6] arrived.

And the newborn child has someone to love and care for them twenty-four hours a day including weekends, because it is a well-known scientific fact that nanas never sleep and know what you are doing ALL the time, which is OK when you are very little but not so great when you are a teenager. Nanas are there until the very second their charge gets married and, in some cases, the young Prince Arthur in particular, they are there forever.

Furthermore, the top-notch nanas, such as those looking after princes and princesses, only look

---

[6]   *Posh word for baby.*

14

after one child. When the child they are looking after gets married, they retire. There is no such thing as a second-hand nana.[7] Of course, the old nanas are not turned out to fend for themselves or made into sausages like they still are in some parts of Eastern Europe. No, they are looked after for the rest of their lives.

So it is at Camelot. High up under the roof of the great west wing is the Attic of a Thousand Nanas.[8] Room after room of little old ladies sitting by small open fires knitting lumpy cardigans and smiling vacantly at cups of cold tea.

But their innocent-looking knitting and tea-drinking hides a dark secret.

Nanas never sleep.

So when Arthur whispered into the darkness, 'Daddy must become dead,' Nana Agnys heard him.

Nana Agnys knew that her beloved charge was too dumb to find his way out of a wet paper bag, and without her help it would be many, many years

---

[7]   *If you don't believe me, see how many you can find on eBay.*

[8]   *There are not a thousand nanas living there, but the builders of Camelot believed in planning ahead.*

15

before he would become King.

The thought of being the King's nana filled her with great excitement. The King's nana was the Top Nana. All other nanas were beneath the King's nana and had to do whatever she asked. The King's nana had first choice of all the knitting patterns. She got to sit at the top table, could kick the servants, and even make fun of Fremsley the Royal Whippet.

She decided she would speak to someone who would speak to someone who probably knew someone who could find someone who wouldn't ask any awkward questions . . . and something would be done.

ARE YOU FEELING DOWN, UNLOVED, SPOTTY AND GENERALLY USELESS? THAT'S PROBABLY BECAUSE YOU ARE. BUT DON'T WORRY. VISIT THE DOWNWIND ISLANDS, WHERE YOU WILL MEET PEOPLE WHO ARE EVEN MORE USELESS THAN YOU ARE. AND ONCE YOU BEGIN TO FEEL A LITTLE BETTER, OUR TRAINED STAFF WILL BEAT YOU WITH STICKS AND THROW YOU IN THE WATER.

The King is dead in several dramatic and exciting ways all at once, though not necessarily in that order. Long live the King.

erlin was in a bad mood. He had been the Top Wizard of Avalon for longer than anyone. He had served some of the greatest kings who had ever lived, majestic figures for whom the word majesty had been created. If anyone asked him who was the greatest king of all, he could never decide. They had been magnificent in so many ways.

Now the days of glory seemed about to fade away. Prince Arthur was everything a king should not be, but less talented. Of course, the boy was only eleven years old and might grow up into a brave, fearless, handsome king like his father, but somehow Merlin doubted it.

'It's true that he does have the legs of a king,' said Merlin to his manservant, Hyssop. 'It's just the bit between his ears that I'm worried about.'

'Master,' said Hyssop, 'he is but a child. By the time our great King Uther-Pendragon passes over the River Styx to the Land Beyond Valhalla,[9] Arthur may have grown into a fine young man, especially

---

[9] *Old-fashioned speak for 'when he's carked it'.*

with your wisdom to guide him.'

'True,' said Merlin. 'But I have a terrible premonition that our King is not long for this world.'

If he hadn't known better, Merlin would have sworn that Arthur was not the son of the great Uther-Pendragon but some changeling, and the real Arthur had been spirited away. He never spoke of this to a single soul, but it was forever in the back of his mind, except on a full moon, when it came to the front of his mind and kept him awake.

Only one other person suspected this had happened and she had good reason. Mouldgrace the Royal Midwife, who had been attending the Queen as she gave birth to Arthur, had popped out to the toilet just after Arthur was born, and when she returned to the Queen's boudoir, she had seen a large black eagle fly out of the window with a bundle of rags in its beak.

That's funny, she thought. *It's Tuesday and they don't usually collect the laundry until Friday. And they usually send an old washerwoman with a basket, not a big black bird.*

Mouldgrace was not the brightest carrot in the

bunch and it wasn't until she mentioned the eagle to Merlin a few weeks later that their secret suspicions were aroused. But they kept them secret. Merlin, because he knew that a day would come when the information would be of great importance, and Mouldgrace, because she had short-term, mid-term and long-term memory loss and had already forgotten whatever it was they had been talking about.

'Except I think it had something to do with sausages,' she said later.

The day after Arthur's birth, Nana Agnys was delivered to Camelot. She knew from the start that something wasn't right about her charge, but hey, she was the nana to a prince. She wasn't going to rock the boat.

Once a month on the full moon, when for some strange reason he couldn't sleep, King Uther-Pendragon would visit Merlin in the long, dark hours of night and, as the two old friends shared a mug of royal cocoa, he would say, 'How could I have fathered such a petulant little brat?'

Merlin thought about telling the King of his suspicions, but never did. He wasn't sure one way or

the other and life was complicated enough without adding any stuff that might not be true. Nor did he mention his premonition about the King's soon-to-be-dead situation.

'Fear not, sire,' he would say. 'When you have passed over the River Styx to the Land Beyond Valhalla, I shall look after the boy.'

'It's not the idiot boy that needs looking after,' Uther-Pendragon said. 'It's my Kingdom.'

'Fear not, sire,' Merlin reassured him. 'You are the King and Avalon is your Kingdom. When your idiot son becomes monarch I will make sure this wonderful land does not become an Idiotdom.'

'You are a good and faithful servant,' said the King. 'Avalon will be safe in your hands.'

'I only live to serve, your majesty,' said Merlin, who actually only lived to serve Merlin.

That had been the last time Merlin and Uther-Pendragon had drunk cocoa together. Before the

next full moon arrived, the great King had died.

He was shot in battle by a second cousin of Nana Agnys, poisoned by a toffee made by Nana Agnys, cut down by a mighty sword that Nana Agnys had been polishing that very morning, bitten by an angry tiger which had once had a very painful thorn removed from its foot by Nana Agnys, knocked down by a runaway team of thirteen horses pulling a mighty war chariot, who were half-crazed from eating fermented straw fed to them by a stable boy who had once had afternoon tea with Nana Agnys, struck by lightning on his lovely silver bracelet (a birthday present from Nana Agnys), cut his finger on a very toxic mushroom that had been growing on a discarded boot that had once been worn by someone who looked remarkably like Nana Agnys, fell off a high castle battlement onto thirty-seven really sharp spikes that Nana Agnys had been meaning to put out for the Camelot Castle Cleanup because they were infected with anthrax, but hadn't actually got round to doing, was seriously frightened by a very big spider which was actually a distant relation of Nana Agnys, and suffocated by not taking a breath while he was

23

reading the longest sentence in this story, all within the space of twenty-seven minutes.

Merlin's fear had been confirmed when a big black crow has crossed the chapel window at midday.

The simple fact of a big black crow flying past the chapel window was not normally seen as an omen of oncoming danger. In fact, Avalon was overrun with crows. But this particular big black crow had been trailing a white banner behind it emblazoned with the words 'The King's a Goner'.

'Gonna what?' said the young Arthur when Merlin told him of the omen.

'No, sire . . .' Merlin began to explain.

'And what's an omen, is it one of those flat yellow things?'

'Flat yellow things, sire?' said Merlin. 'Do you mean the sun?'

'No, no, stupid. The flat yellow things people have for breakfast. With that delicious-smelling bacon,' snapped Arthur.

'Oh, an omelette?'

'Yes. Is it like one of them?'

'No, sire.'

'So the King's not gonna have some breakfast?'

'No, sire,' said Merlin. 'In truth, I fear it means the King has had his last breakfast.'

'Gosh,' said Arthur. 'So you mean he's going on a diet?'

'Almost right,' said Merlin. 'It is diet, but without the "t" at the end.'

'Oh yes, I can understand that,' said Arthur. 'I prefer coffee at breakfast too.'

Merlin thought that by the time he managed to get the boy to understand exactly what was happening, the Earth would have crashed into the Sun and the entire solar system would have vanished in a puff of dust. So, like always, he agreed with the last thing Arthur said and then left the room to find a peasant to bang his head against.

By the time he returned, the great King Uther-Pendragon was dead, the complete idiot boy Arthur was King and the Dark Ages had begun.

Whenever Merlin talked to Arthur, the conversation always went in a strange, surreal direction, so he tried to spend as little time with the boy as possible. The trouble was that now that

Arthur was King, contact would be unavoidable. Thoughts of revolution, running away and murder began to grow in Merlin's mind, but his promise to Uther-Pendragon and his knowledge that Avalon must survive no matter what made him determined to do as much as he could to keep the new King under control.

Merlin was the most magical person in the Kingdom, the only true wizard, though his talents in that direction were not so much based on him being a mystical superhero as the fact that he was the owner of the only copy of *The Wizard's Big Book of Spells*.[10] Where this book had come from, no one knew. The first spell he had cast when he had got the book was to make every other copy of the book turn into a small pair of socks.

The Wizard's Big Book of Spells was a treasure trove of magic, from a spell to turn a cow into a raspberry to seventy-three spells on how to make various things invisible. One of them nearly cost Merlin his power because it made the book itself

---

[10] *Which may or may not someday be made available to EVERYONE, including you, as an exciting, yet terrifying, picture book.*

invisible and Merlin had a terrible time trying to find it again. Luckily there was a undo button inside the front cover. And although the book's owner could make a beautiful eight-horned flying unicorn out of nothing more than a mug of pond weed, two warts and a Welsh miner's helmet with a lamp on, there wasn't one single spell that would allow Merlin to make young King Arthur wise or modest or nice.

Even with Merlin's awesome powers stretched to their limit, the future for Avalon did not look good.

The Far Away Toilet that time and the cleaners forgot.

I t was happening again.

It was the ninth time in ten days and King Arthur was furious. This, of course, was exactly why they were doing it.

'Nana!' roared King Arthur at the top of his voice, but no one came.

This was because King Arthur's voice was not very tall, so even when it stood on tiptoe it only sounded like an undernourished three-year-old girl having a tantrum. Not only that, but the toilet that Arthur was sitting on was in the Gruelling Tower, one of the most remote parts of the castle, where very few people ever went. There were lots of bits of Camelot that no one ever visited, either because they were too cold or too haunted or because the decor was really bad.[11]

The Gruelling Tower, where the King was sitting, was all three. He was the only living person to have been there since Lord Minivere deVere had

---

[11] *On the other hand, there were people who not only visited but actually lived in these damp, remote places. We might return to them from time to time, though probably only when we are having nightmares. See page 107.*

29

been frightened out of his skin by the ghost of his granny, who wasn't actually dead, while he had been sitting on the exact same toilet. That had been over a hundred years ago, but bits of Lord Minivere's skin were still stuck to the wall.

The 'it' that was happening again was bubbles. They were coming up through the drains and exploding in the toilet bowl. The smell was horrible and the King recognised it immediately.

Dragon breath.

Whichever toilet the King sat on it happened.

He had assumed that the dragons were doing it to everyone, but they weren't. It was just him. He had tried using different toilets – that was why he had gone up to the Gruelling Tower in the first place – but it hadn't made any difference. Somehow the dragons managed to blow their bubbles up into whichever of Camelot's two hundred and fifty-three toilets he was sitting on.

'Nana!' the King shouted again, but once again there was no response.

He tried to stamp his feet on the ground, but his legs were too short so all he could do was bash his heels against the toilet bowl. Unfortunately he had forgotten he was wearing his toad-stomping boots, the ones with the steel plates down the back, and the toilet shattered, dumping him on the floor in a big puddle.

In the years since the toilet had been last used, the toilet paper had been carried off by mice. It was only now that the King realised this. He went through his pockets, even though he knew he was far too important to carry anything in them. In fact, he thought that because he was the greatest King in the world, he was far too important to have anything as common as a pocket in his clothes, and yet there they were – three of them. He made a mental note to have the seamstress who had put them there sent to L'île de Pain Grillé,[12] where he had decided he would send all his enemies to visit the Burning Salamander, but right now he had more pressing matters. Except there was nothing to do the 'pressing' with. He

---

[12] *Which is French for The Island of Toast, but sounds much grander. Unlike anyone who is sent there, we may return to L'île de Pain Grillé.*

31

looked around the tiny room, but there was no paper anywhere.

It fact the only thing he could use was the bits of Lord Minivere deVere's skin – and even that kept tearing as he peeled it off the walls.

So after he had marched back down to the occupied parts of Camelot, in an even sulkier mood than normal, he had to have four baths in puppy's tears before he felt clean again.

'Even the spiders were laughing at me,' he complained.

'Surely not, sire,' said Merlin, who knew which side his bread was buttered on.[13]

'Oh yes they were,' sulked the King.

'Oh no, sire, no one laughs at you,' said Merlin. 'Everyone loves you. They say you are the greatest King ever, far greater than your father.'

'You are such a crawler,' said Arthur. 'Do they really say I'm greater than my father?'

'Indeed, sire,' Merlin lied. 'And you have a much nicer name.'

---

[13] *This was dead easy. Neither side of his bread was buttered because only the King and Fremsley the Royal Whippet were allowed to eat butter.*

'Well, yes, that's true. I mean, King Arthur sounds magnificent, doesn't it?'

'Verily, sire.'

'And Daddy's name was just silly. I mean, who ever heard of anyone called Uther-Pendragon,' said the King. 'For goodness sake, he couldn't even spell Other properly.'

'Absolutely.'

'And who was the main Pendragon anyway, if Daddy was the Other one?'

'Quite so.'

'And Pendragon? What sort of name is that? Was Daddy a dragon who had a pen? I don't think so,' said Arthur. 'I mean, dragons haven't got any thumbs so they couldn't even pick up a pen, never mind write a letter with one.'

'Indeed, sire. Your great insights and wisdom only confirm that you are the greatest King of all time,' said Merlin, adding the bit of flattery that he knew would make Arthur pink with joy. 'And, as all the ladies agree, you have the handsomest legs in all the Kingdom.'

Whenever the boy got angry or upset, Merlin

suggested some nice new clothes to show off his perfection. This always sent Arthur rushing to the nearest mirror to admire himself and so calmed him down.

'Yes, I do, don't I?' said King Arthur.

'Without a doubt, sire,' said Merlin, wondering how much more of this self-important, nasty little boy he could take.

'One[14] thinks,' said the King, 'one thinks the Embroidery Ladies of Camelot shall make one a new velvet tunic with flowers of diamonds to celebrate this wonderful day, and the Royal Portrait Painters shall record it for all to see.'

'What day is that, sire?' said Merlin.

'Why, Thursday, the day that is named after me,' said the King. 'Though of course it should really be called Arthursday.'

'So true, sire.'

New clothes always put the boy in a good mood

---

[14] *Like a lot of self-important kings and queens, Arthur frequently referred to himself as 'one'. Really he should have called himself 'one-quarter', which would have summed his personality up much more accurately, but then the same could be said for anyone calling themselves 'one'.*

34

so everyone made sure he got them several times a day. As he fantasised about a new tunic more splendid than any other tunic ever made, he remembered the pocket problem. That put him in a bad mood again, and the bad mood made him remember why he had discovered the pockets in the first place, and that meant he had to go and have another bath and, having had five baths in less than an hour, his skin went wrinkly and that put him in a class one bad mood, which was the sort of mood where he threw things out of the window. Today's mood was so bad that it wasn't until he had chucked sixteen kittens, a small chair, and four turtle doves in a pear tree out into the moat that he began to calm down. Of course, the turtle doves didn't so much fall into the moat as fly away.[15] Fortunately Merlin managed to distract the King so he didn't notice, otherwise it would

---

[15] *It should be noted here that, unknown to the King, Merlin had arranged kitty trampolines below the castle windows. While this did not stop most kitties falling into the moat, they did bounce up and down a lot before they did. Apart from being really funny to watch, this made Merlin a lot of money from betting on how many times a kitty would bounce before it flew off into the water. DO NOT try this at home. See page 177.*

35

have been yet another of those days.

Most people have some special talent. Admittedly it might be for something fairly modest like peeling an orange really, really fast without squirting any of the juice in your eye. Most kings' talents usually involve killing more people than anyone else. After all, this is how their ancestors became king in the first place.

King Arthur's greatest talent, the one thing he did better than anyone else at Camelot, was sulking with a side-order of foot stamping. Although his ancestors had been good at the killing and conquering stuff, after he was born and his parents saw what an idiot he was, they made very sure he did not inherit or learn a single warrior-like trait.

'Can you imagine it?' King Uther-Pendragon had said. 'He'd kill people because they were prettier than him or had shapelier legs or didn't like mauve.'

So the great Merlin had cast a spell over Arthur to keep him as meek and mild and lazy and vain as a Persian cat. 'But without the killing small defence-less animals bit that cats do all the time,' King Uther-Pendragon had requested.

Merlin cast the spell and thus it was that after Uther-Pendragon died and Arthur became King, it was Merlin who ran things, though he always made sure Arthur thought he was in charge.

Thus it was ever so, thought Merlin, who had actually been running things for a very, very, very, very long time.

The sulking was an unwanted side effect of Merlin's control spells, but he reckoned it was a small price to pay.

The Dragons of Camelot and the surrounding valleys, a couple of mountains, some very dark caves and a secret place behind a big tree,

'**R**oarin' thumbs.'

'What?'

'Thumbs. If we had thumbs,' said Spikeweed, 'we would be the ones in charge. It'd be us in that castle, not stuck here in these caves in this horrible bleak valley surrounded by even more horrible bleak mountains where even the grass won't grow.'

'Yeah, yeah,' said his wife, Primrose, who had heard it all a thousand times before.

'Stands to reason, doesn't it?' Spikeweed continued. 'I mean, we're a hundred times stronger than humans. We're much bigger and ancienter. We're better looking and we have enormous brains. And answer me this – out of dragons and humans, only one species can breathe fire. Who's that then? For goodness sake, how can you breathe fire and not be in charge? I'll tell you how. Roarin' thumbs. It's all down to the roarin' opposable digit.'

'Do you need to swear so much?' asked Primrose.

'Of course I do,' said Spikeweed. 'It's one of the

things dragons do better than any other species. No, it isn't, is it? Even roarin' humans swear more than we do.

'And,' he added, 'on top of all that, they can't even roarin' fly. Chuck a human off a castle wall and what do they do, soar away with the grace of an eagle? I don't think so. More like soar away with the grace of a lump of mud.'

'Yes, yes,' said Primrose. 'We all know. There's no justice in the world.'

'Too right,' Spikeweed whinged. 'Too right.'

'But no one ever said there was,' said Primrose. 'There was no promise of fair play. You can't get your money back.'

'Oh yes, rub it in, why don't you?' said Spikeweed. 'You try picking up small gold coins when you haven't got thumbs.'

He then proceeded to shout the fourteen-thousand-and-fifty-seven swear words that every dragon learns as soon as they hatch. It made him feel a bit better to know that even though humans swore a lot more than dragons, they didn't have nearly so many bad words to use.

'Why don't we make ourselves false thumbs?' said their son, Bloat.

'Because, stupid, to do that would require a manual dexterity that we lack because we haven't got thumbs,' said Spikeweed. 'I'm going outside to burn a puppy.'

'It's your own stupid fault there's no grass, you know,' Primrose shouted after him. 'If you didn't keep burning everything we'd have lovely green trees and soft grass and flowers and butterflies and all that sort of stuff, everywhere, not just charcoal-covered rocks.'

'I hate butterflies,' Spikeweed muttered as he left.

Spikeweed was the King of the Dragons. He was to dragons what Arthur was to humans except he wasn't vain, spoilt or stupid like Arthur.[16] Also, unlike Arthur, who was often happy in the same way a stupid bouncy labrador puppy is happy, Spikeweed was in a bad mood every minute of every day, awake

----

[16] *Actually, he was vain and stupid, it was only his 'spoilt' that was different from Arthur's. Arthur's 'spoilt' meant everyone gave him whatever he wanted. Spikeweed's 'spoilt' meant ruined.*

or asleep. It wasn't always about thumbs, though it usually was about not being in charge.

He came from a long line of dragon kings, a line that went back far further than Arthur's. But now Spikeweed, his wife, Primrose, their son, Bloat, and their other child, whose name they kept forgetting, were the last of the line of pure-bred royal dragons. There were plenty of other dragons dotted around the world, but none of them had the proper original vintage royal dragon blood. They were just your common or garden peasant dragons, even those jumped-up Italian dragons who called themselves Counts and the rubbish German dragons who called themselves Barons. Compared to Spikeweed and his family, all the others were just big flying lizards.

When Spikeweed's son, Bloat, got married in the future, his wife would not have proper pure royal dragon blood and the world of dragons would probably, maybe, perhaps decay into a world of democracy.

'One dragon, one vote,' moaned Spikeweed. 'It doesn't bear thinking about.'

The dragons' days of glory were long behind

them. They had reached their peak when they had shared the world with dinosaurs. Soon sorted them out, hadn't they? As Spikeweed had already pointed out, only one species could breathe fire. The smell of burnt dinosaur that had filled the air for nearly a hundred years had proved that. Archeologists mistakenly thought that the dinosaurs had become extinct because of a giant meteorite crashing into the planet. That was how they explained the thin layer of burnt stuff they kept discovering whenever they dug up old fossils. But no, Spikeweed's ancestors had been the bringers of fire, not some hot rock falling out of the sky.

The most famous joke in dragon society[17] went like this:

'What do you call a brontosaurus after a dragon has turned it into toast?'

'I don't know. What do you call a brontosaurus after a dragon has turned it into toast?'

---

[17]   *This is the only joke in dragon society.*

43

'**A burntosaurus.**'

There were two other endings to this joke:

'**Itneversaurus.**'
and:

'**Breakfast.**'

Then creatures with thumbs had evolved and that had been the beginning of the end. Thumbs meant they could make things and most of the things early humans had made had pointy ends. Pointy ends are made to be stuck into creatures without thumbs and, dragons being very large examples of creatures without thumbs, they had lots and lots of pointy things stuck in them until they were nearly extinct. Thumbs also gave humans something to suck when they felt frightened about being cornered by dragons when they didn't have a pointy stick with them.

'Maybe it's because we can't read,' said Primrose, who realised she was becoming as miserable and pathetic as her husband. 'Maybe there's an instruction book on how to be in charge and if we could read it,

then we could take over. Though of course if there was a book, we wouldn't be able to read it, because we couldn't turn the pages. We could read the cover, I suppose, except dragons can't read. It's not fair. I mean, we're huge and magnificent. We should be happy, not depressed. Your father's right. Roarin' thumbs.'

'I wonder,' said Bloat, 'whether if we wait long enough, we'll evolve thumbs.'

'I doubt it,' said the other child, whose name they kept forgetting. 'And by then all the other species would have probably died out so if we made pointy things, we'd be the only ones left to stick them into.'

'Depressing, isn't it?' said Bloat.

'Oh, you remembered at last.'

'Remembered what?'

'My name.'

'Did I?'

'Yes.'

'Remind me again?' said Bloat.

'Depressyng. It's Depressyng.'

'I know, but what's your name? I've forgotten it again.'

45

'Depressyng,' said Depressyng.

'Right. I think I'll go and help Dad scorch a few rocks,' said Bloat.

Primrose went to the back of the cave where Spikeweed's grandmother, Gorella, was sleeping. It was more like hibernating than sleeping. All the ancient dragon ever did was lie curled up on her bed of dead thistles, snore and endlessly wet herself. Once or twice a day she woke up and talked to things on the wall that weren't there. And once or twice a week, she limped and shuffled out of the cave into the afternoon sunshine to bask on a rock.

If there wasn't much to keep an old dragon occupied, there was even less for a young dragon to do. Damsels to capture and make distressed were few and far between, which meant there were very few knights looking for a fight. When the dragons had discovered the old tunnel under the moat that led into the sewers below Camelot, it had looked as if it might open up all sorts of possibilities to finally overthrow the humans, but the castle was protected by dozens of Anti-Dragon Spells, so all they could do was blow bubbles up the drains into the lavatories.

'Not much of a career for a young dragon, is it?' said Bloat to Depressyng as they puffed out their cheeks for a really big breath. 'When I nod my head, we'll both blow together. I'm fed up with making bubbles. Let's see if we can get a bit more action.'

'It could be worse,' said Depressyng. 'At least it's the King we're bubbling at.'

From far above them came a scream followed by a curse as King Arthur was blasted off the toilet. He was thrown upward so violently that he hit the ceiling. His crown embedded itself in the plaster before crashing down in a shower of plaster all over him. He was angrier than anyone could remember and ordered the Master at Arms to drop a large bomb down the toilet.

'Incoming!' shouted Depressyng and the two young dragons ran back down the tunnel as the bomb exploded behind them.

The bomb was not a good idea. It landed in the main sewer and exploded. Big bombs in narrow tunnels have only one outcome. The entire sewer collapsed in on itself, blocking every single toilet and drain in Camelot.

Of course, no one realised for a few days. They just kept flushing, pulling out the bath plugs and pouring things away down the sinks that were too disgusting to eat or drink,[18] just like normal. When they finally realised that the drains were blocked, it took a while to work out why and that made it worse. No one was going to dare blame the King.

'What is that awful smell?' he demanded. 'Everyone must have a bath immediately.'

'But, your majesty, the drains . . .' Merlin began.

'IMMEDIATELY!'

'But . . .'

'And then they must have another bath.'

'Sire, please, sire, may I speak?' Merlin pleaded.

'Not until you've had a bath,' Arthur ordered.

---

[18] *And don't forget, this was in medieval times, when people would happily eat cockroaches and drink stuff they squeezed out of dead worms. So you can imagine what the stuff they wouldn't eat was like. Actually, you probably can't, and if you can, you need therapy.*

After Merlin had sat in a bath of filthy water that had been used by at least twenty-seven other people and Fremsley the Royal Whippet and his pet armadillo, Petunia, he drenched himself in cologne and went back to the King.

'It would appear, your majesty,' Merlin finally managed to say, 'that the sewers have collapsed and are totally blocked.'

'Did you say sewer?' snapped the King.

'Yes, sire.'

'How dare you say that word in front of me. Do you not know that I am the most sensitive and exquisite creature in creation and I am at a very impressionable age? Why, the mention of that word has so tarnished my ears that I must have a bath immediately.'

'Oh no, your majesty, no, no . . .'

But it was too late. All the bits of King Arthur that had been sparkling clean like a white porcelain figurine were now a nasty shade of grey and greasy with little bits of chewed beetroot stuck everywhere. Being a superstitious child, Arthur assumed someone had cast an evil spell over him, so he had another

bath in a different room. This merely added a lot of dog hairs to his sticky coat because he hadn't looked on the bathroom door and had used Fremsley the Royal Whippet's bathroom. A third bath filled in the remaining gaps on his body with second-hand muesli.[19]

Then the King was angrier than he had been the time when he had been angrier than he had ever been before. He was throw-fifty-kittens-into-the-moat angry, and even after that he was still angry. The only way to get truly clean was for him to stand on top of one of the tallest towers for a whole hour while Merlin made a cloud come and empty itself on him. Even then he didn't feel truly pure and beautifully clean.

'What are we to do?' he asked Merlin. 'Surely you can perform some magic to clear the drains?'

'I am a wizard, sire, not an engineer,' said Merlin. 'The drains are not so much blocked as totally collapsed.'

---

[19] *As someone who would make muesli illegal if I were King, I have always thought it looked second-hand even straight out of the packet. How can anything that had no fat and no sugar be any good for you?*

'Why?'

'Someone threw a bomb down a toilet, sire,' said Merlin.

'Who on earth would . . . oh, um,' said Arthur, going a rather fashionable shade of red. 'What are we to do?'

'Well, sire, the only way into the drains is through the secret tunnel that your great-great-great-grandfather's great-grandfather built,' said Merlin.

'So send some men along the tunnel to fix it.'

'Unfortunately, sire, the entrance to the tunnel is at the back of the cave where the dragons live. No human could reach it alive,' said Merlin. 'They would be charcoal before they even got inside the cave.'

'What about a monkey?' said Arthur.

'I fear a dragon would think a monkey was a very small hairy human.'

'A goat?'

'Sire, I imagine any living creature would suffer the same fate,' said Merlin.

'How about a not-living creature, um, say, a zombie?'

'Still toastable, sire.'

51

'One has just had a brilliant idea,' said Arthur. 'An idea so brilliant that even you, the greatest wizard ever, did not think of it first.'

'Indeed, sire?'

'Yes, armour,' said the King. 'We need a bold and courageous and fearless knight in a suit of fireproof armour.'

'Methinks, sire, that as well as bold and courageous and fearless, this knight would need to be stupid too,' said Merlin. 'Unless of course a very large reward was offered.'

'Brilliant. What shall we offer this brave knight?'

It so happened that King Arthur had a sister, Morgan le Fey. She was many things that Arthur was not, including intelligent and quick-witted. She did have some things in common with her brother, but they were things that looked much better on her, which made Arthur hate her. Her long blonde hair was longer and blonder. Her lovely face was lovelier and she had two really gorgeous legs, so gorgeous they even looked good in tartan tights. She was also something Arthur most certainly was not. She was twenty-one and grown-up.

'How about the hand of your sister, the Lady Morgan le Fey, sire?' Merlin suggested. 'I would imagine that even the most cowardly knight on earth would take on a hundred dragons for the chance to marry so beautiful and wise a princess.'

Merlin hated Morgan le Fey too. She questioned every single thing he did, even down to the colour of the paint on the handle of the paint cupboard. If Merlin could get her married off, preferably to someone who lived a very long way away, it would solve a lot of his problems.

In her turn, Morgan le Fey hated Merlin. She knew Arthur was as bright as a very small torch with a broken bulb and a totally flat battery and he was way too useless to manage a small puppy, never mind an entire kingdom, but she hated the way Merlin controlled everything. If anyone should have been in charge it was her.

The trouble was that Morgan le Fey was ferociously independent and not about to marry anyone she wasn't in love with.

But a few well-placed spells should be able to fix that, Merlin thought, though he had to admit

none of his spells had ever worked on her in the past.

Never mind, he thought. *We'll cross that drawbridge when we come to it.*

'Let there be Royal Messengers sent to every corner of the Kingdom,' said King Arthur, 'calling for a Brave Knight to carry out this noble deed. Let them come with the speed of lightning because one simply cannot bear another day using a bucket as a lavatory and having to stand on the roof in the rain to get washed.'

'It might be best to leave out the bit about the toilets being blocked up,' said Merlin. 'Probably better just to say there are some ferocious dragons that need slaying.'

'All right.'

'And probably better to leave your sister's name off the proclamation. Just say the hand of a beautiful princess.'

'Yes.'

'And probably offer several big bags of gold too, your majesty,' said Merlin.

'My thoughts entirely, good and faithful wizard,' said Arthur. 'You know, it never ceases to amaze me

how you seem to be able to read my every thought.'

'Indeed, sire,' said Merlin. *Or actually create them,* he thought.

So it was decided that the next morning four Royal Messengers would set off to ride to the four corners of the Kingdom.

There was no time to lose. The three-hundred-and-forty-seven buckets dotted around Camelot were almost full and every single bucket shop for a hundred miles in every direction was totally sold out of buckets, except for the Environmentally Friendly Bucket Shop, whose buckets were made of recycled grass and were therefore one hundred per cent useless due to leaking, falling apart and getting eaten by goats.

The quest begins rather slowly and some naughty spies are revealed.

'My spies tell me,' said Spikeweed, 'that King Arthur is sending messengers out on a quest.'

'What spies?' said his wife. 'You haven't got any spies.'

'Have too.'

'You're really sad, you know,' said Primrose. 'You live in fantasy land.'

'Well, no. I am Spikeweed, King of the Dragons, not sad at all, actually,' said Spikeweed.

'King of the Dragons? King of what? A damp cave in a miserable valley with a population of five: you, me, the kids and your senile old grandmother. Some kingdom.'

'We shall rise again,' said Spikeweed unconvincingly. 'You just wait and see. I have plans.'

'Get real.'

'Yes we will, and I do so have spies.'

'Well, if you're so clever how come you can't even dry this cave out?' said Primrose. 'You can go outside and turn the whole valley into a waste-land with your macho fire-breathing, but you can't

get rid of the damp in here.'

'I thought you liked it damp,' said Spikeweed.

'What?'

'I thought you liked the slime running down the walls and all the mould growing everywhere,' said Spikeweed. 'I think it's romantic.'

'Oh yes, every young wife's dream is this place,' sneered Primrose. 'When my mum said I was going to marry the King of the Dragons, I imagined something a bit better than this. I tried to be realistic. I wasn't expecting a castle with crystal spires and all the puppies you can eat, but I certainly thought it would be better than this disgusting hovel and a diet of earthworms. It wouldn't be so bad if your grandmother didn't live with us. The smell of mildew's bad enough, but the awful stink of a leaky old dragon's wee is unbearable. I spend all day in here with my eyes watering.'

Spikeweed looked desolate. He had assumed that, because he was the King of the Dragons, every other dragon, especially his wife, adored him. Now it turned out the only one who did adore him was his ancient granny, Gorella, and she was so far out of it

that she didn't know who or what her grandson was. In fact, she spent most of her time talking to a green stain at the back of the cave thinking it was her dead husband.

But one thing Spikeweed was right about were his spies. It was them who had told his children which toilet King Arthur was sitting on and it was them who now told him that the King was sending out messengers to find a knight brave enough to come into the dragons' cave to enter the secret tunnel that led to the collapsed drains.

Primrose still wouldn't believe him, though. 'These spies are in your head,' she sneered.

'So you do believe I've got spies then?'

'What are you talking about?'

'You said my spies are in my head and they are. Look,' said Spikeweed, tilting his head and giving it a shake.

Three cockroaches fell out of his ear.

'See,' said Spikeweed. 'These are my spies, Adam, Evel and Barry.'

'You're kidding.'

'No,' said Spikeweed. 'They are the perfect

spies. They can fly all over Camelot in and out of every room and cupboard and drawer and spy on everyone. Take a bow, boys.'

The three cockroaches flew up onto Spikeweed's left shoulder and bowed. Primrose was speechless. Maybe her husband was not quite as big an idiot as he looked, though at four hundred and fifty kilos he was seriously big.

'Maybe I misjudged you,' she said, trying to see him in a new light. 'I just thought you were a complete dork when in fact it's all a cunning disguise.'

'Yup,' said Spikeweed, drawing himself up to his full height and puffing out his chest.

His full height was actually taller than the cave so the illusion of majesty was rather spoilt when he bashed his head and sent a pile of rocks crashing down, one of which flattened Barry. Cockroaches hate waste so Adam and Evel picked up the bits of Barry and ate them.

No, he is as big an idiot as he looks, Primrose thought.

'My cunning disguise is to lull the humans into a false sense of security,' said Spikeweed. 'They think

that we are dumb and powerless when in fact we are very cunning and . . .'

'Powerless,' said Primrose.

'That's what we want them to think,' said Spikeweed.

'And they're completely right.'

'Um, no, er, it's just a cunning disguise while I work on my plans.'

'Ooh, and what plans are those then?'

'They're secret. I'm still working on them,' said Spikeweed, 'but you wait and see. When I am ready I shall send out the call and all the other dragons around the world will come and join us and we will once again rule the world.'

'Once again?' said Primrose. 'And when did dragons ever rule the world?'

'A long time ago.'

'Oh right, and I suppose part of this ruling the world involved almost becoming extinct, did it?'

'No, that was, um, that was because of, er, those, um, them dinosaurs,' said Spikeweed. 'They done it, but we winned because they all got extincted and we didn't.'

'Great. Well, your majesty, while you're formulating this incredible plot to overpower the unsuspecting humans and gain world domination, could you drag your granny outside into the rain and wash her down? The smell is making my eyes water so badly I can hardly see a thing.'

Apart from the stupid red bump on top of your head, she thought.

Adam and Evel were only two of dozens of cockroaches that spied on the humans for Spikeweed. But because cockroaches have no scruples at all and are basically evil and even go and suck your toothbrush at night while you're asleep,[20] they will spy for anyone. As well as spying for King Spikeweed, the Camelot cockroaches spied on the dragons for Merlin, spied on Merlin and the King for Morgan le Fey and even spied on each other for each other. As long as there was cake involved they didn't care who they spied on. In the case of the dragons, they had made an exception to the cake rule because, apart from the very rare Gateau Dragons of Patagonia, dragons do not have cake. However, by an amazing

---

[20] *Well, they do in my house.*

62

fluke, dragon's earwax tastes exactly like cake, so they had made a deal with Spikeweed that in return for somewhere warm and cosy to sleep – his ear – and all the earwax they could eat, they would spy for him.

Romeo Crick, son of some dead peasants, lowest of the low and the least likely person to ever become a superhero.

Romeo Crick knew nothing of the world upstairs or the luxury of having a bucket to cherish and call his own.

Living, as he did, deep in the sculleries below the main kitchens of Camelot, he knew very little of anywhere.

Romeo Crick was eleven years old, the same age as King Arthur. They were both slight, good-looking boys with blond hair and big blue eyes, but every tiny thing of their two lives could not have been more different.

Upstairs, the young King lived a life of total spoilt luxury. He not only had fresh mauve tights for every day of the week, he had fresh mauve tights for every hour of the day and a special mauve tights servant whose only job was to make sure his master had an endless supply of fresh mauve tights.

Below stairs, Romeo Crick had never even seen a pair of tights. All he had to cover his legs was a layer of mud. Nor did he get a new layer every day. The one application, scraped from the drains below

the kitchens, had to last a whole month.

Romeo Crick had lived in the sculleries since he had been bought at a midden sale at the age of five.[21] During the past six years he had washed and trimmed the stalks and leaves of more than seventy-five-thousand beetroots, for Romeo Crick was Camelot's Beetroot Leaf Preparation Operative, though he did dream of the day he would be promoted to washing the actual beetroots and pass his job on to someone below him – if ever there was someone below him.

For this work Romeo was rewarded with a pallet of straw to sleep on, two potatoes and a knob of gristle each day. He was also given a slice of bacon every Christmas and would have been given another slice on his birthday, except he wasn't, because no one knew when his birthday was.

Even the rats looked down on Romeo Crick, and they kept eating his bed.

Romeo came from a poor family in a poor

---

[21] *Midden sales are like garage sales only with a lot more mud and body parts. Romeo Crick may have been a large three-year-old or a very small fifteen-year-old. No one, including Romeo himself, knew his exact age so they stood him next to other children and decided he was about five.*

village where luxuries such as beetroots were but a distant dream and shoes were a rumour that no one actually believed. The villagers were so poor that even the air belonged to someone else and many of them simply died because they couldn't afford to breathe. When the infant Romeo had been washed up on the bank of the river in a wicked basket,[22] most of the villagers thought he was a fish.

'Don't be stupid,' said Molly Crick, who was to raise Romeo as her own. 'It's a little baby.'

'No, no, 'tain't possible,' said the villagers. 'It come out of the river so it must be a fish. Babies doesn't come out of a river. A big bird brings babies.'

Molly unwrapped the baby and held him up in the air for all to see, but they still didn't believe her.

''Tis a miracle,' everyone said. 'A fish that looks exactly like a baby.'

Then they spent two hours deciding the best way to cook a fish that looks like a baby until Molly's husband, Unthank Crick, threatened to kill anyone who laid a hand or a filleting knife on his new son.

---

[22] *Which is the same as a wicker basket but with nasty sharp bits.*

'Anyone tries to dip him in batter,' he warned, 'and I'll batter them.'

Molly and Unthank didn't have any children, so they didn't care if Romeo was a fish or a boy or a fish boy. They were going to raise him as their own.

After that the rest of the village tended to keep away from the Crick family. Even when the crops failed and everyone was forced to eat grass for every meal instead of just breakfast, Unthank Crick would allow no one near his precious child. There were murmurings that it was the fish boy who had brought the drought and made all the dandelions and turnips wither away, but Unthank was the biggest and strongest man in the village so Romeo was safe. Unthank was also the second-biggest and second-strongest *person* in the village as Molly Crick was a good head taller than her husband and could lift him over her head with one hand. It would be many years before Playstations, televisions, computers and electricity would be invented, and watching Molly Unthank lift her massive husband above her head and then juggle him and two potatoes was the village's most popular Saturday night entertainment.

'Must be wonderful to be so strong,' said all the women, their eyes full of admiration.

'Must be wonderful to own two whole potatoes,' said all the men, their eyes full of envy.

Times were hard in the village and as the months passed they got harder. The Cricks were forced to eat their potatoes, and juggling with two lumps of mud and a slug just didn't excite people the same way.

'At least we can console ourselves with the fact that things can't possibly get any worse,' said the village headman as a crow flew off with the slug.

But he was wrong.

That night the evil Angry Knights of Twilight[23] razed the village to the ground. They carried off all the women, thinking they were rather attractive sheep, killed all the men, thinking they were rather ugly sheep, made glue out of the children, ate the babies and knitted the kittens into doormats.

Only Romeo, Unthank and an old pig called

---

[23]   *Who were terrible, but not as terrible as the Angry Knights of Darkness.*

Geoffrey survived, because they had all been bathing in the sewage pit during the attack.[24]

'Oh well, at least we've still got each other and our health,' said Unthank to Romeo after the Knights of Camelot had driven the Angry Knights of Twilight away. 'And at least there's no one left who would like to deep fry you.'

Unfortunately this was the last thing he said because seven seconds later a flock of dragons had burnt what was left of the village and Romeo's father to the ground.

Romeo Crick and Geoffrey had survived because they had been sitting up to their necks in a puddle while everything around them turned to ashes. The puddle had not actually belonged to Romeo or Geoffrey, but as its owner had been killed by the Angry Knights of Twilight, they had moved in and claimed it for themselves.

'Oh well, at least we've still got each other and our health,' said Romeo to Geoffrey.

And our lovely puddle, thought Geoffrey.

---

[24] *Just to clear up any confusion, Romeo and his father had been bathing in the sewage pit. Geoffrey had been standing at the side holding their clothes and fallen in.*

Unfortunately this was the last thing Geoffrey thought because seven seconds later a bolt of lightning struck the pig between the shoulder blades.

It was the incredibly appetising smell of roast pork that had attracted the passing travellers who had rescued Romeo Crick. The travellers had not so much rescued the boy as stuffed themselves full of roast pork before stuffing him into a sack, dragging him off and slipping him into someone's midden sale while they weren't looking. That had been the last time Romeo had seen the light of day.

The Cook from Camelot had paid five groats for Romeo Crick.

'And that's only because it is a very good sack,' she said as she handed over the money without looking inside the sack, but hoping there might be a new turnip inside.

It wasn't until she had got back to the kitchens of Camelot and turned the sack upside down to shake out any spiders that she'd realised Romeo was inside it. Her first reaction at not finding a turnip was to throw him into the moat.

However, by a wonderful coincidence, that

71

was exactly what had happened to the miserable wretch who had been Camelot's previous Beetroot Leaf Preparation Operative. One of the cleaners had swept him up with the dirt. He had been so puny and half-starved that when she went through the dirt to salvage the nourishing bits to add to the soup – dead beetles, scabs and such – she hadn't seen him. So he had, like so many kitchen boys before him, become Krakatoa the olm's dinner.

Thus it was that Romeo Crick became the new Beetroot Leaf Preparation Operative and the first boy to actually think it was a great job. The glorious purpleness of the stalks was like poetry to his soul. After washing and polishing thirty thousand leaves it all seemed a bit less exciting. Beetroots just didn't seem quite so magical any more.

Having survived three fires, it would appear that Romeo was luckier than everyone around him, but that wasn't the case. There was another reason that Romeo had survived the fires, but it wasn't until he was pushed into the kitchen ovens that he, or anyone, realised it.

The seventeen great ovens in the kitchens of

Camelot were as tall as a man and as old as the castle itself. In fact, two of them were several hundred years older. They had been part of the castle that had stood in the place where Camelot now was. Apart from the two ovens, this ancient building had collapsed and, quite a huge number of years later, King Arthur's ancestors had said, 'Wow, look at that pile of stones, let's build a castle.'

In the Derelict Years, as that time between castles came to be called, seven monks had lived in the two deserted ovens. They had remained there while Camelot had risen around them and would probably be there to this day if the new Cook hadn't said, 'I reckon those two brick tunnels would be great for cooking pizza.'

'But what about the monks who live there?' someone had said. 'Are they not sort of sacred?'

The Cook did not believe in that sort of thing and shortly afterward invented Pizza Monkeretta, which has evolved into the modern Pizza Margherita.[25]

The seventeen ovens were heated with burning

---

[25] *Every good book and TV show has a cooking segment. See page 231 for a Camelot Pizza recipe.*

73

coals and gradually clinker formed on the bricks. It built up until so many bits kept falling into the food that the Cook could not get away with pretending they were black pepper and someone had to crawl into the red-hot furnaces to rake it all out. So the post of Official Clinker Raker was created. The wages were awful, the days were long, but the job did have one thing in its favour. Yes, the days were long, but there weren't very many of them. No Official Clinker Raker had ever managed to clean all seventeen ovens before they had become clinker themselves. In fact, the largest number of ovens cleaned out by an Official Clinker Raker was about one-tenth of one.

'We need to find a more efficient way of doing this,' said the Cook as her assistant swept up the little pile of charcoal that had once been called Arnold Blight. 'I mean, we're running out of small boys.'

'I know, Cook, we got a dozen new ones on Friday and that was the last of them.'

By an incredible coincidence the Cook's eye fell on Romeo Crick, who had fallen asleep in the middle of a mountain of beetroot leaves. She picked up her eye, pushed it back into its socket and hauled

Romeo up by the scruff of his neck.

'HOW DARE YOU FALL ASLEEP ON THE JOB, YOU LITTLE WEASEL!' she screamed into his ear.

Before Romeo could point out that he had actually only been allowed three minutes rest in the past week due to a huge influx of fresh beetroots, the Cook dragged him over to one of the ovens, shoved a rake into his hand and threw him inside.

'CLEAN!' the Cook roared.

So he did.

He walked to the back of the oven and began scraping. All around him, the floor, the walls and the arched roof glowed orange with the heat. Even though she was standing several metres away from the mouth of the oven, the Cook could feel her eyebrows melting. Yet Romeo Crick, deep in the heart of the inferno, was totally untouched. His clothes caught fire and fell off him, but he was unmarked. Not one single hair on his head was scorched. His skin glowed as gold as the fire, but he wasn't even sweating.

After half an hour he had cleaned the entire oven and jumped out with a big smile on his face.

'Is this a promotion?' he said as the Cook gave him a beetroot leaf to cover himself with. 'Do you want me to clean another one?'

Everyone gathered round him, touching his skin in disbelief. If they hadn't seen it for themselves, no one would have believed it. They had all seen a small, skinny boy climb into a red-hot oven and climb out half an hour later without so much as a tiny red mark on him. Romeo Crick was fireproof.[26]

'You know, ma'am,' he said to Cook, 'if you made me some pastry trousers I could cook them while I was cleaning.'

He then cleaned three more ovens before lunch, which made it a day Romeo would remember for the rest of his life.

'Not the four ovens,' he would say later, 'but lunch. That was the first time in my life I ever had lunch. I had three pie crusts and a whole carrot all to myself.'

After that, Romeo Crick was treated like a hero. The Cook went to her Spare Kitchen Boy Cupboard and got a new child to become Camelot's Beetroot

---

[26] *Do you see a crafty link forming here?*

76

Leaf Preparation Operative. Romeo's bed was moved from his damp hole in the wall to a drawer in the bottom of a kitchen cabinet — not the rough cabinet where the old saucepan lids and cracked jam jars were stored, but the big dresser where the best knives and forks were kept. He had pie crusts for lunch every day after that and as many knobs of gristle as he wanted whenever he wanted. And so it was that the weedy child who had looked like a pencil on a diet gradually put on weight and grew stronger.

The Cook, who had never married or had children, began to look upon Romeo as her own son. Unfortunately adoption hadn't been invented in those days, otherwise she would have taken him as her own child. Fortunately adoption hadn't been invented in those days, otherwise she would have taken him as her own child and the poor boy's name would have been changed from Romeo Crick to Romeo Bladder.

The Cook told her kitchen staff that under no circumstances were they to tell anyone above stairs about Romeo's talent.

'If this gets out, they'll take him away from us,'

she said. 'So if I find anyone has breathed a word, they will become casserole. Understood?'

Everyone nodded. They all remembered what had happened to Dym Trotter. No one wanted to follow in his footsteps, though they had to admit his footsteps had been delicious.

Of course, an incredible talent such as Romeo's could not stay secret forever, no matter what the Cook said. It was a talent that would set him on a new career path, leading to fame, fortune, a pair of clean tights for every day of the week and big boots with very pointy toes. But for now, Romeo, with his very own drawer to sleep in, was happier than he had ever been in his life.

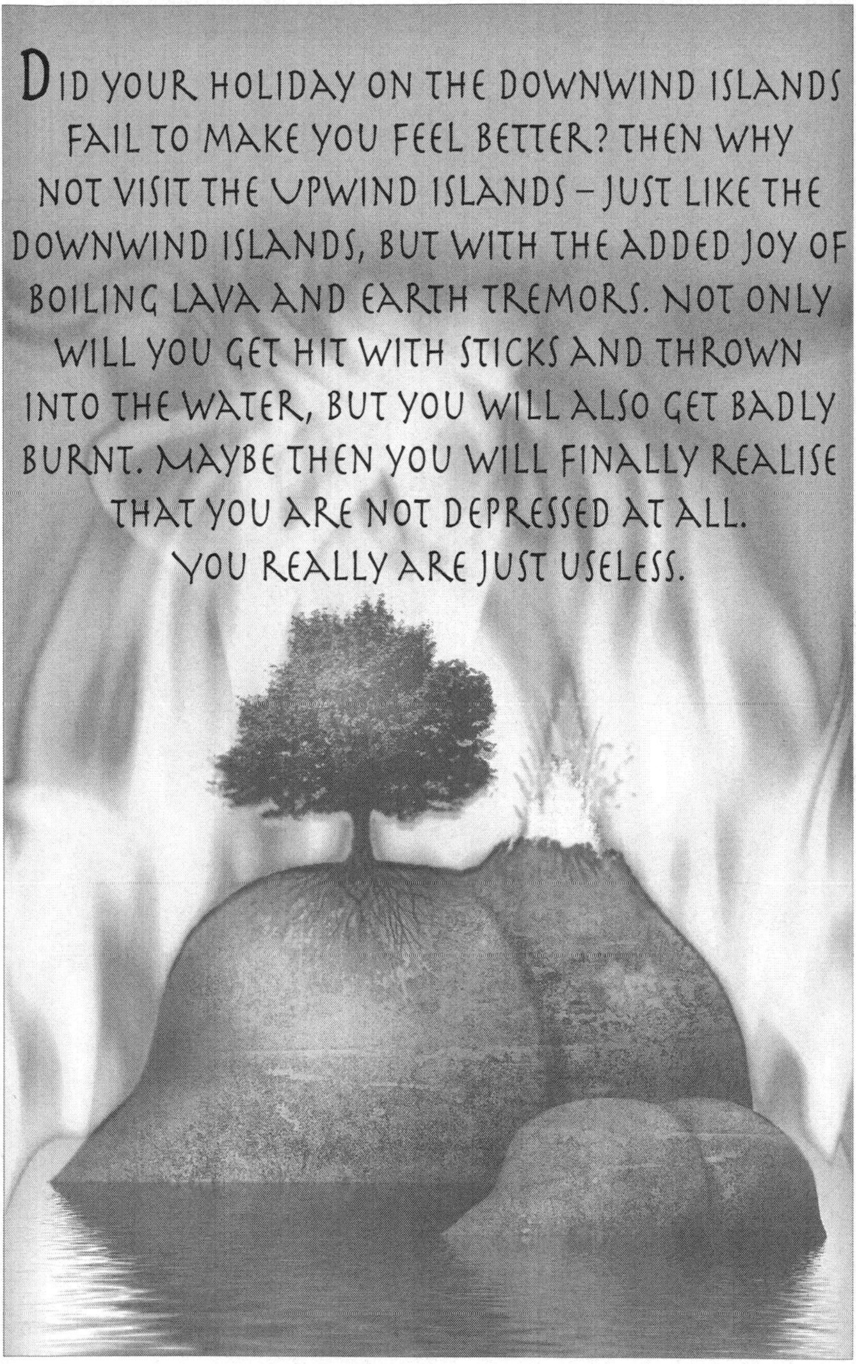

To the distant corners of the Kingdom and Beyond and a very tall cliff just past Beyond.

Heaven

Ye North

BEYOND

The Welsh Place

Ye East

The Place That No One Talks About

King Arthur's Kingdom was called Avalon and it stretched as far as its borders in all directions. Camelot was at the very heart of the Kingdom. Originally a damp, windswept land full of miserable ignorant Celts, the great wizard Merlin had transformed it by magic so that in King Arthur's time it was covered in endless beautiful mountains and valleys and flat bits with windy rivers and lush green fields full of strawberries and tomatoes that actually tasted of something.[27] It was a truly beautiful and idyllic land where everyone lived in complete peace and harmony except for those people who didn't. It was heaven on earth except, unlike heaven, you didn't fall off if you went too close to the edge.[28] Unfortunately when

---

[27] *Strawberries.*

[28] *Unless of course you went to the Very Tall Cliffs of Asgirth, stood on the Very Slippery Grass of Asgirth and tried to look down at the Very Pretty Puppies of Asgirth, who always played right at the foot of the cliffs. Then you most definitely would fall off, but generally not get killed due to your fall being cushioned by the Very Pretty Puppies of Asgirth, who were extremely soft and cuddly until you fell on them, when they became extremely soft and flat.*

81

Merlin finally died some centuries later in 1927, the magic wore off and the land became, once again, a damp windswept place full of miserable ignorant Celts.

'Oh great Royal Messengers,' began the King. 'Well, one says "great", but of course I'm the only person who is really great, but then as you are my own messengers I hereby decree that you shall be called great while you are doing my messenging. Oh great Royal Messengers, I charge you – and when I say charge, I don't mean you have to pay me anything – I mean, one hereby commands or orders you to search my glorious Kingdom for brave and fearless knights who will come to our aid.'

'Indeed,' said Merlin.

'Of course, one is braver and fearlesser than any knight and one would love to go and fight the dragons oneself, but unfortunately that is not possible for technical reasons,' the King continued.

He did not explain what the technical reasons were. Nor did anyone dare ask him, but they all knew. The King was a pathetic coward who was scared of paper bags and didn't want to get his tights dirty.

'May our blessings be with you, together with a packed lunch and thirty-five groats,' said the King. 'And for the Royal Messenger who finds the Brave Knight who completes this great quest, there will be a wonderful reward.'

He did not explain what the wonderful reward would be, but everyone knew. King Arthur's wonderful rewards were usually a set of dinner plates depicting famous heroes of Avalon who were all King Arthur. They also got a tabard[29] with 'The Totally Incredible King Arthur Gave Me This' embroidered on it. Most people who got the wonderful rewards sold them on YeBay, which was like eBay before computers and electricity and involved a lot of carrier pigeons. It could take months to place a bid, never mind actually buy or sell anything.

So the four Royal Messengers set off on their quest, galloping like the wind on their trusty steeds across the great drawbridge towards the seventh island. Four days later, they had managed to cross the other six islands and reached the mainland. It had been a particularly crowded time on the bridges

---

29   *A kind of ancient version of a hoodie.*

and it had really slowed them down. The Royal Messengers had had to push at least fifty people into the moat simply to get by.

But at last they reached dry land and were ready to set off on their quest.

The first Royal Messenger, Sir Barkworth, rode East.

The second Royal Messenger, Lord Pleat of Perivale, who had picked the shortest straw, rode as slowly as he could towards Wales. Maybe, he thought, one of the others will find the Brave Knight before I get there so I can go home.

The third Royal Messenger, Sir Lamorak, rode forth and North at the same time.

And the fourth Royal Messenger, Sir Bedivere, rode West.

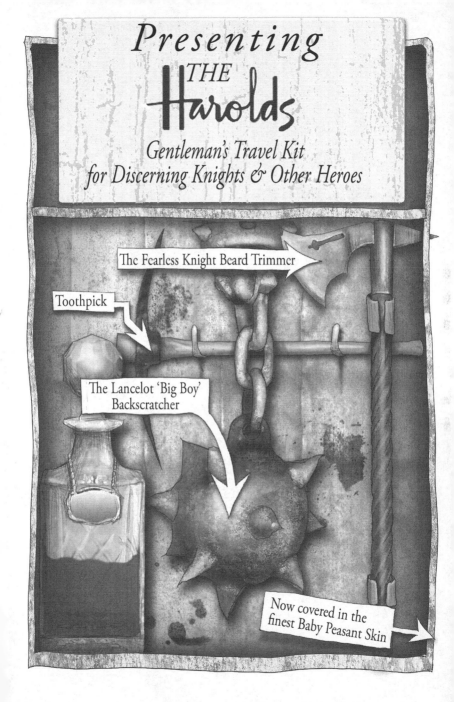

Presenting
THE
Harolds
*Gentleman's Travel Kit
for Discerning Knights & Other Heroes*

The Fearless Knight Beard Trimmer

Toothpick

The Lancelot 'Big Boy' Backscratcher

Now covered in the finest Baby Peasant Skin

How to make
babies the dragon
way, which of
course has
no rude
bits in
it at all.

When a bird hatches from its egg, it can't fly. This is usually because it hasn't got any feathers. Some birds, even when they do grow feathers, are still rubbish at flying. This includes:

- *Emus – too big and heavy.*
- *Ostriches – even bigger and heavier.*
- *Chickens – too stupid.*
- *Turkeys – too big and heavy AND stupid.*
- *Kentucky Fried Chickens – too cooked.*
- *Rabbits – not a bird.*

Dragons are the same except they don't have feathers. When a baby dragon hatches out from its egg it can barely stand up, never mind walk about or get off the ground. The trouble with baby dragons is that they are even more stupid than chickens, and as most of them hatch out in nests in the tops of very big trees, they stay stupid for quite a long time due to the concussion from falling out of their nests and landing on their heads.

This is part of the natural order of things. Nature has evolved the dragon so that it grows far

too big to fit in its nest a long time before it learns to fly. This way baby dragons spend at least the first six months of their lives staggering around seeing stars and wondering why their heads hurt. The reason for this, as all human children know, is that it is very dangerous for little children to play with fire, and as dragons can shoot flames out of their noses as soon as they hatch,[30] it's important to keep them distracted as long as possible. Concussion does this. Now and then there are accidents with lazy baby dragons who don't want to leave their nest. What happens then is they breathe fire, burn the nest and fall on the ground. The end result is the same except they have burnt skin as well as concussion.

Young Bloat, son of Spikeweed, King of the Dragons, was one of these. He had burnt his feet so badly that he had to spend the first six weeks out of the nest with his legs tucked under his leaky great-granny Gorella while they healed. This, of course, scarred him for life, as it would anyone who spent a month and a half with their legs soaking in old

---

[30] *There was a species of dragon that could breathe fire while they were still inside their shells. Of course, this made hard-boiled eggs and the species became extinct.*

dragon's wee.[31] Fortunately the concussion protected him from his great-granny's endless wittering about nothing as she talked to the wall, though he did have very strange dreams and developed an allergy to walls that he never got over.

Primrose was not happy when her son was hatched. First of all, the little sod had set the nest on fire, which meant she would have to build another one if she ever wanted to have more children, which she did. Second, she dreaded the future, when her very weird son might one day become King of the Dragons after Spikeweed passed away.

'Though it wouldn't surprise me if Bloat sets himself on fire before he even grows up,' she said. 'And as for all the stress of building another nest when I haven't got thumbs, well, I just don't want to talk about it.' Dragon nest building is a very long and complicated business. Birds generally have

---

[31] *In Bellingen, the town I live outside of, there is an island that is home to seventy-thousand flying foxes. When it rains, the smell of bat pee as you drive by is overwhelming, but people living nearby hardly notice it. This has absolutely nothing to do with Bloat, who even now curls up and begins to whimper at the slightest hint of pee fumes.*

quite delicate beaks that allow them to pick up twigs and weave them together. Dragons have big lumpy mouths with dreadful teeth and such bad breath that a lot of twigs simply rot away before they can carry them up to the top of the tree. Also, they need to build really big, strong nests because they are big and heavy creatures. The standard nest-building technique is to blast away at the foot of a tree until it catches fire and falls over. This has do be done just before a rain storm otherwise the whole tree will get burnt. If the rain starts just as the tree falls over, it will put out the fire and the dragon is left with a nice big pile of smashed-up branches.

Bloat had been hatched in Primrose's first nest and it had taken her fifteen goes before she got it right. The thought of going through it all over again had been very depressing. She had sat at the mouth of the cave watching a winter storm lash down over the valley. All the burnt grass turned to black mud that even the endless lightning couldn't make look attractive. She remembered the lush green valley of her childhood and the happy days when she was a young carefree dragon dreaming, like all her friends,

of meeting a dragon prince and living happily ever after.

Then she had met Spikeweed and it had all been downhill ever since. Sure, she had been the only one of her crowd who had actually married a prince, but the happily-ever-after bit seemed to have been held up in the mail.

I should have married Spotty Oregano, she thought. *He might have only been a humble Italian dragon of lowly birth, but he had lovely eyes. I bet he's living happily ever after all the time.*[32]

The second nest had been a lot easier and when her daughter had been born, Primrose had thought she would be happy at last. Now she would have someone to share her hopes and dreams with. The trouble was that her hopes were few and far between and her dreams were really depressing, so her daughter did her best to avoid her. That was why the poor child had been given the name Depressyng.

---

[32] *He wasn't, actually. When Primrose had turned him down he had become a monk, the first dragon to do so, and was now living in a ditch in a remote monastery in Silesia unable to think of anything but the image of his lost love.*

Morgan le Fey – more beautiful than a bucketful of chocolate, more clever than a whole box of very clever owls yet wonderfully modest.

Morgan le Fey lived in the North-West Wing of Camelot. It was her domain and no one apart from her few faithful servants was allowed there. She had ordered the castle builders to remove all access to the wing except for one very narrow winding corridor, a corridor so narrow that people visiting Morgan le Fey had to walk in single file and weigh less than eighty kilos.

'I hate people in twos and I hate fat people in ones,' she said to Lady Petaluna, her lady-in-waiting.

But most of all, Morgan le Fey hated her little brother, King Arthur, and with good reason. In fact she had so many reasons to hate him that if she had written them all down, it would have taken her so long that she wouldn't have had any time left to do the actual hating.

She didn't just hate him because he was as stupid as a wooden spoon in a bonfire. She hated him because in spite of his stupidity and only being eleven years old, he had still been made King when their father had died, simply because he was a boy

and she wasn't. This, of course, is a fine, old and totally unfair tradition still used in many countries around the world to this day.

It's probably the main reason there is so much trouble in the world, she thought. *If girls were in charge, there's be a lot less fighting stupid wars.*[33]

She hated Arthur because he was vain, sulky and stupid. He was very stupid, more stupid than the average eleven-year-old boy, extremely stupid and total world stupid champion. The trouble was that, like a lot of stupid people, he thought he was clever, which meant that almost every decision he made was a bad one.

'If it wasn't for that wizard Merlin protecting him,' she said to Lady Petaluna, 'our enemies would have conquered us a long time ago. I'm just glad that I am immune to the wizard's magic.'

(Because Avalon was the most beautiful kingdom in the world and Camelot the most beautiful castle and it had the greatest wizard ever, and the sun shone all the time, even when it was raining, most of the

---

[33] *On the other hand, there would probably be even more Hello Kitty, pink glitter and reality TV shows.*

kingdoms surrounding it hated it and its King and Merlin.

'They think they are so wonderful with their pretty butterflies and beetroots as big as cabbages,' said King Ingeborg of Norway, 'but we've got things they haven't.'

'True,' said his wife, Queen Outaborg. 'Like frostbite and blizzards and cabbages the size of beetroots.'

'Well, our wizard is better than theirs.'

'Oh yes, mighty Thumblik can turn water into ice,' said the Queen. 'Hooray.'

King Ingeborg's father had tried to invade Avalon once, but it had been a disaster. The 'narrow stream' he had ordered his army to wade across had turned out to be the North Sea and those who hadn't frozen to death had been knocked out by large icebergs and drowned.)

'But is not our King Arthur a wise and wonderful ruler full of wonderfulness and wise wisdomness?' said Petaluna, who was blinded to the King's stupidity by his beautiful mauve tights.

'My child, although you are wise beyond your

years,[34] you are blinded by my brother's beautiful mauve tights,' said Morgan le Fey. 'It is true they are beautiful, but you are being misled by the magic of the colour mauve. For, as everyone knows, mauve has an awesome power over people. That's why my brother will let no one else wear it.'

It might seem that Morgan le Fey was not a very nice person, and if you are spoilt and stupid then you definitely wouldn't like her, but in fact she was as kind as she was beautiful, as beautiful as she was clever and as clever as she was kind. It was just that she had no time for fools and Camelot seemed to have more than its fair share of them. The nicest people were mostly at bottom of the food chain and the higher up you went the more useless they became, culminating in Morgan le Fey's brother King Stupid. So Morgan preferred the company of servants and gardeners to that of so-called great knights and teachers. The servants had nothing to prove. They had little to lose and felt no need to impress anyone, whereas the knights lived in constant fear of being exposed as the useless parasites they were. They had

---

[34] *A whole seven months beyond her years, in fact.*

everything to lose and because Morgan le Fey made no secret of the fact that she could see right through their pompous pretences she was not popular in Court. She was accused to being stuck-up, which was exactly the opposite of what she really was, but as it meant most of the people she despised avoided her, she was quite happy for them to see her that way.

'I dream of a world where the people are as lovely as our beautiful Avalon,' she said. 'Not on the outside, I mean, but inside their heads. But I suppose while my brother is King that is unlikely to happen.'

Historians have pointed out that Morgan le Fey was probably the world's first hippie, especially when her tomb was discovered in 1976 and her coffin was draped in a coat of many colours with the words 'Love and Peas' embroidered on it in gold thread.

As Morgan le Fey had said, Lady Petaluna was just a child. She was eleven years old and had been Morgan le Fey's lady-in-waiting for the past five years. Queen Igraine had acquired the child in a cart boot sale in a box of pig's bladders. Lady Petaluna had been in the box playing with the bladders and no one had noticed her until they got back to Camelot

and then no one could be bothered to take her back. A messenger had been sent to her parents. A few gold coins had changed hands and Lady Petaluna had been given to Morgan le Fey as a maid.

Fortunately Morgan le Fey, apart from hating people in twos, fat people in ones, stupid people in any amounts and her brother and quite a few other people too including Merlin, was a kind and lovely young woman and took Lady Petaluna under her wing, treating her almost as if she was her younger sister, apart from making Petaluna sleep at the foot of Morgan le Fey's bed on a pallet of straw and not giving her a crown to wear.

Over the ensuing five years they had become devoted to each other. Lady Petaluna trimmed her mistress's toenails and in her turn Morgan le Fey allowed Petaluna to sell the clippings on YeBay. Lady Petaluna removed unsightly hair from parts of her mistress's body where they were not welcome and in return was allowed to use the hairs to make herself a lovely comfortable pillow which, after four years of resting her head on a rock as she slept, was wonderful.

Because she was a Top Royal Princess, there

were many places in Camelot that Morgan le Fey could not go, either because they were not very clean or they were listed in her *Princesses' Guide to Camelot* as banned. Of course, if Morgan le Fey had decided to go somewhere that wasn't considered proper for a princess, no one would have dared to stop her. Apart from her sharp tongue, she also had a sharp sword, which she was rumoured to be incredibly good at using.

Lady Petaluna, however, had free rein to go wherever she liked, from the dungeons deep below the kitchens to the Attic of a Thousand Nanas and even up to the remote tower where Etheldred the Wise Woman lived. So it was that Lady Petaluna became the eyes and ears of Morgan le Fey. The child was a lot more reliable than the cockroaches, who tended to tell people what they thought would bring them the greatest reward.

'Of course, as the King's sister, I should be allowed to go everywhere,' Morgan le Fey complained.

'Oh no, my lady,' said Petaluna, 'there are places no one would want to go.'

'Like where?'

99

'Down in the dungeons.'

'Have we really got dungeons?' asked Morgan le Fey.

'Indeed, my lady, and they are terrible to behold,' said Petaluna.

'And are there prisoners there?'

'There are and they are terrible to behold.'

'And you have beholded them?' Morgan le Fey, whose governess had been rubbish at teaching English, asked.

'I have and they are terrible to hear. They wail faint and low,' said Petaluna. 'And they are terrible to smell. They smell strong and high.'

'But they must have been there forever,' said Morgan. 'I mean, my brother hasn't caught any prisoners. He's too scared to say boo to a goose, never mind fight any wars or battles.'

'They have been there many, many years,' said Petaluna. 'Word has it that some were there before your father became King.'

'That's terrible,' said Morgan le Fey. 'We must do something.'

'I have done something, my lady.'

'What, you mean you've helped them escape? How brave of you.'

'Well, no, not that, my lady. They are all still there,' Petaluna explained. 'But I have brought them good cheer and sustenance.'

'How?'

'I took each one of them a marmalade sandwich and some cabbage water,' said Petaluna.

'Oh.'

'Yes, my lady,' said Petaluna. 'I have made a friend in the kitchens and he helped me.'

'A friend? Surely not a common kitchen boy?' said Morgan le Fey.

'Indeed, my lady,' said Petaluna, 'But he is a special boy, not like the other half-starved wretches down there. I hardly dare say it, but he has a majestic air about him, a natural dignity I have never seen before. And he has a great talent that I believe no other living person possesses.'

'This boy, what is his name?'

'He is called Romeo Crick, my lady.'

'And this talent that has so impressed you, what is that?' said Morgan le Fey.

101

'He is fireproof.'

'Now what have I told you about telling lies?' said Morgan le Fey.

'No, no, my lady, it's true,' said Petaluna. 'I have seen it with my own eyes.'

She told Morgan how she had seen Romeo climb into a glowing-red oven and clean it. He had been in the oven for fifteen minutes and when he had come out he had been completely unscathed. She also told her mistress how the Cook had made her swear on the *Royal Cookery Book* not to tell a soul about it.

'And now that you have told me,' Morgan le Fey ordered her, 'you will make that promise again, only this time you will keep it. You will not tell a single soul. If you do, my love for you will vanish and be replaced by a very sharp pointy stick. Understand?'

'Yes, my lady.'

'Good girl.'

Even though she couldn't stand to be in the same room as her little brother, Morgan le Fey knew that he had sent Royal Messengers out to scour Avalon for a Brave Knight to confront the dragons

and go through their cave into the secret tunnel that led to the blocked drains under Camelot. She knew, too, that any knight – even the legendary Lancelot, whom she had never met, but who sounded as if he might actually be a true and wise knight and not at all a twit – would get burnt alive by the dragons long before they could reach the tunnel.

She also knew that her brother had promised her hand in marriage to any knight who was successful.

'We'll see about that,' she said. 'He may be the King, but if he thinks he can make me marry anyone he likes, he's got another thought coming.'

'Oh my lady, how could you defy the wishes of the King?' said Lady Petaluna.

'With a very sharp pointy knife,' said Morgan le Fey. 'A secret knife that even that evil old fool Merlin cannot protect him against.'

Lady Petaluna was terrified. She adored her mistress, but the idea of her murdering the King was dreadful.

'Of course, if – and there are a lot of ifs – there was a Brave Knight who did manage the task, and if that Brave Knight was called Lancelot, and if Lancelot

was as stunningly handsome as this tiny engraving of him which I got free with a year's subscription to *Handsome Knights Monthly*, and if Lancelot was as incredibly intelligent, brave and witty as the article in the magazine suggests, well, then, and only then, I might actually, possibly, maybe consider becoming his wife.'

But Morgan le Fey knew all these ifs were unlikely to happen. There were just too many of them. She also realised that the information about the humble kitchen boy was priceless. It was unlikely that a knight would be found who could take on the dragons. Even with the latest advances in armour technology, anyone foolish enough to try to get past the dragons would end up as Boil-in-the-Can Human. Of course, without thumbs, the dragons wouldn't be able to get the knight out of his armour to eat him, but he would still be roasted alive.

But a boy who was fireproof?

It was too good to be true.

So Morgan le Fey decided she had to get Romeo Crick out of the kitchens and into the North-West Wing before her brother found out about him.

'Roughly how many prisoners would you say there are locked in the dungeons?' she asked Petaluna.

'I would say, my lady, that there are thirteen,' Petaluna replied, 'and I would say they are all roughly.'

'And who knows they are down there?'

'You, me, the kitchen boy and the jailer,' said Lady Petaluna.

'So we can assume the kitchen boy won't talk about them or else he'd get into trouble for stealing the marmalade sandwiches and the cabbage water,' said Morgan le Fey. 'So that just leaves the jailer. What's he like?'

'His name is Clynk and he is not happy, my lady.'

'And why is that?'

'He has been like a prisoner too, my lady,' Lady Petaluna explained. 'His father and grandfather were the Royal Jailers before him. He was born down there and has known no other life. He has never once seen the light of day. It is as if he himself is a prisoner. The only difference is that he is on the other side of the cell doors.'

'So he yearns for freedom as do the prisoners?'

'Indeed so, my lady.'

'Can you take me down to the dungeons?'

'Oh, my lady!' Lady Petaluna cried. 'How could someone as fine and beautiful as you even think of going to so vile a place?'

'I shall disguise myself as a common serving wench and you shall take me down to the dungeons and then to the kitchens that I may see this Romeo Crick for myself.'

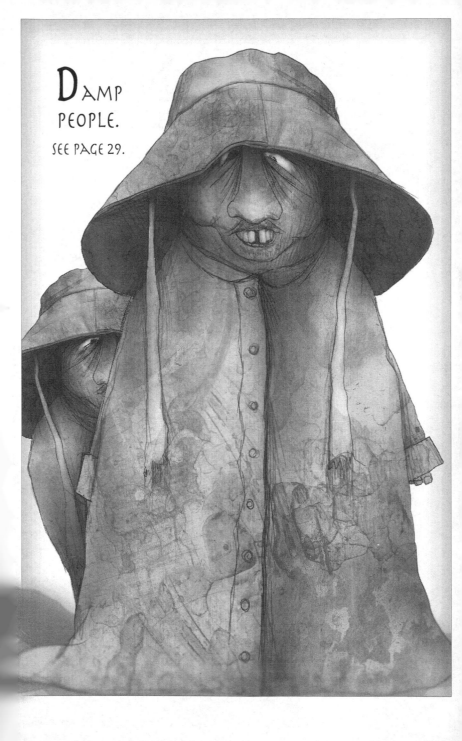

Damp
PEOPLE.
SEE PAGE 29.

Sir Barkworth's journey to The East via Cloud-Cuckoo Land.

Of the four messengers the King had sent out, Sir Barkworth was the most useless.

Sir Barkworth Barkworth de Vere Rissole Rustington of Barkworth the Younger, to give him his full title, had more letters in his name than brain cells in his head. He was one of the Cloudy Knights, which meant he was like a night when clouds cover the sky and there is nothing to see. He was an example of the ridiculous tradition, still carried on today, that says if your father was a lord then, no matter how stupid and useless you are, you are a lord too. He had all the right qualifications – no chin, very large ears and he spoke in a silly voice that had nothing to do with the way words were actually spelt.[35]

Sir Barkworth Barkworth de Vere Rissole Rustington of Barkworth the Younger had inherited the title from his father, Barkworth Barkworth de Vere Rissole Rustington of Barkworth the Little Bit Older, who had in turn won the title as a consolation prize in a raffle, apart from the Sir bit, which Barkworth the Younger had earned when he

---

[35] *See page 151 for some examples of how to talk Orfly Posh.*

had removed a splinter from King Arthur's big toe. It had been a really agonising splinter and Barkworth the Younger had managed to remove it painlessly by using an anaesthetic – a sudden bang from behind on the King's head that had made him unconscious. When the King came round and discovered his foot wasn't hurting any more, though he did have a bit of a headache, he was so grateful he knighted Rissole on the spot and gave him seventy-six groats a year for life and a complete set of dinner plates featuring the famous heroes of Avalon.

The Barkworth Barkworth de Vere Rissole Rustingtons of Barkworth have two claims to fame that are still with us today. Most people know that the sandwich was named after its inventor, the Earl of Sandwich, but few know the the rissole was named after Sir Barkworth. The family's second claim to fame is that the phrase 'barking mad' is named after them too.

Being a deeply committed coward, before being volunteered to be a Royal Messenger Sir Barkworth had been the Court Coat Holder. This involved hiding behind a very large rock or tree and holding

everyone's coats while they fought their battles. He was so good at this job that even the King's enemies would get him to hold their coats too.[36]

Lords generally address each other as My Lord So and So, especially when they are speaking to Lord Saughandsaugh of Cricklewood, but none of them could bring themselves to talk to Sir Barkworth like that. He was just too stupid. So to everyone, even the humblest kitchen servant, he was known as Woof-Woof.

'I say, Woof-Woof, old chip, trim my toenails, would you? There's a good fellow,' the other knights would say in the same tone of voice they used when asking their dogs to fetch a stick. And, even though he was not clever enough to be called 'stupid', Sir Barkworth had a happy nature that was exactly the same as the dog who had just fetched the stick. So he always did whatever they asked.[37]

---

[36] *This might seem surprising to us nowadays, but in those days there was a lot more chivalry about and, after all, everyone wore a coat.*

[37] *Because nail clippers had not yet been invented, the toenail trimming involved a lot of kneeling on the ground and nibbling with his teeth.*

King Arthur liked to surround himself with people like Sir Barkworth because they made him feel extremely clever.

But no one was sure why the King had chosen Sir Barkworth to be a Royal Messenger. A more useless person to send out on a quest was hard to imagine. There were days when it took him until lunchtime to find the door out of his own bedroom. These were the good days, when he had actually managed to find his bedroom the night before and not had to sleep in a damp corridor with only his manservant as a pillow. This meant that, quite often, by the time he got to the castle dining hall, he had missed breakfast and lunch, and by the time he found his seat he had missed dinner too. There was a joke around Camelot that if anyone wanted to lose weight they simply had to go on the Barkworth Diet.

Yet for all his failings, Sir Barkworth was one of those people who life has blessed. No matter what happened to him, he always landed on his feet. This was easily explained by the fact that his feet were a lot heavier than his head, which was fairly empty. In fact, if it hadn't been for his heavy feet and his big

heart, he would probably have risen into the air and floated away, though of course with his endless good luck, he would have drifted down to earth in a field of chocolate-covered strawberries.

When he had crossed the final bridge to the mainland Sir Barkworth took out his orders and read them several times. They said:

1. *Ride East.*

2. *Find a Brave Knight.*

3. *Turn round 180 degrees.*

4. *Ride back.*

5. *Don't forget to bring the Brave Knight with you.*

'Right, which way's East?' he said, looking for a signpost.

There was a single signpost and it said: 'The North'.

113

However, there was not one which said 'The East'.[38]

'Um, tricky,' said Sir Barkworth. 'This needs some thought.'

Thinking was not one of Sir Barkworth's friends. In fact they barely knew each other and were seldom in the same room together. On the few occasions they were, Sir Barkworth was in the far corner while thinking headed for the door. If they did meet it usually ended in a headache and tears.

Luckily Barkworth had his squire, Nymrod, to look after him. Had he not, his lordship would have got lost before he even found his horse. You would imagine that the last thing a young squire would want after leaving squire school was to work for an

---

[38] *I lived in England for a very long time and in England there are lots of signs that say 'The North'. As a small child I assumed there was a town called The North and I used to wonder why we never arrived there even though we often drove towards it. I now realise that The North is a strange legendary place where all the rainbows end. There were nowhere near as many signs saying 'The South' or 'The West' and I don't remember ever seeing a single sign saying 'The East'. Of course, we might have actually been living in The East, but in fact I don't think The East had been invented when I was young. My favourite place, and one I still think of quite often, was The South-West.*

idiot like Sir Barkworth. But Nymrod was not your average squire. He had been the brightest pupil at squire school, certainly bright enough to realise that being very clever could place him in extreme danger. After all, the bravest knights always had first choice of the new squires, and obviously the bravest knights were famous for being the bravest by exposing themselves to the greatest dangers. On the other hand, a stupid knight would never be trusted with anything important so would be far less likely to get into any trouble. This was proved by the fact that very few brave and fearless knights lived much past thirty, but there were quite a few stupid and cowardly knights who were well over eighty.[39]

So Nymrod acted as dumb as possible in the hope he would end up with the most useless knight of all. He made sure he got every single question on every single test completely wrong, including the one where you had to write your name. On that line he wrote: *No thanks, I've got one already.*

And it had worked perfectly. When all the

---

[39] *In England there is a big house where all the old doddery knights are kept. It's called the House of Lords.*

115

knights had chosen their squires, Nymrod was the only one left. Sir Barkworth had been the last to choose on account of having got himself trapped in the toilet and having taken three days to find the door, quite an achievement in a room only two metres square. Nymrod knew that the greatest danger he or his master would be likely to face would be pricking their fingers collecting wild roses for one of the Court Ladies.

Sir Barkworth got out a pencil and a piece of paper and tried to draw a diagram.

'Oh no, the pencil's run out.'

Nymrod took the pencil and turned it so the sharpened end was pointing at the paper.

'Try it now, master,' he said.

'Wow, brilliant. Right, now leave this to me,' said Sir Barkworth, unwisely.

But a squire always has to do what his master commands so Nymrod sat down beside the moat while Sir Barkworth scribbled and calculated and chewed his pencil and tried to think and failed and scribbled some more. Then Sir Barkworth climbed back on his horse, adjusted his head so it pointed

directly in front and rode straight into the moat.

'Who put that there?' he said as he and the horse scrambled out onto dry land before the olms could get them.

'I think, master, that although you probably did some brilliant calculations, you did make one tiny mistake,' said Nymrod.

'Do you think so?' said Sir Barkworth. 'I doubled checked all my sums. Where do you suppose I could have gone wrong?'

'I think, master, that you probably should have sat on your horse facing the end with the head on rather than the one with the tail.'

'Ah, yes, you could be right,' said Sir Barkworth. 'Jolly complicated things, horses, aren't they?'

'Indeed they are, master,' said Nymrod as they finally set off towards The East.

By then it was getting dark so fifty metres down the road they stopped for the night. They did not take rooms in an inn. There wasn't one. They did not put up a tent. They didn't have one. They simply stopped in the middle of the road and fell asleep in their saddles.

It rained during the night and it rained on the knight.

'Gosh, that was handy,' said Sir Barkworth when they woke up. 'Won't have to waste time having a wash.'

'Indeed, master,' said Nymrod as he wrung Sir Barkworth out.

As they left the valley and rode into new and exciting bits of Avalon, Sir Barkworth wondered if and when he would ever see his home again.[40]

'I wonder, master,' said Nymrod, 'if we shall ever see our homes again.'

'Well, I've never actually seen your home, so probably not,' said Sir Barkworth. 'And to tell the truth, I can't remember what mine looks like. Got a door, I think, and a bit of a roof and some window thingies. And if memory serves, think there might be a couple of sprogs and of course my beloved, um, er, hairy thing, barks a lot?'

---

[40] *Of course he didn't. What he actually thought was,* Hello grass, hello sky, hello horse's ears. *But his horse thought it and also thought,* All these years serving the Kings of Camelot and I end up carrying someone with less brains than my saddle. It's not fair. *His saddle thought,* No one ever said life was fair.

118

'A dog?'

'No, no, the um, the good lady wife, yes, er, Lady Barkworth. What were you saying?'

'Nothing, my lord.'

'Quite so.'

They rode on in silence until they came to a field of sheep, which Sir Barkworth insisted on greeting one by one.

'Fine fellows,' he said as they continued their journey.

That night they did stop at a wayside inn – The Pickle and Coughdrop – where, as luck would have it, there were four Brave Knights also in residence.

'I say, you chaps,' said Sir Barkworth, 'I am by way of sort of being a Royal Messenger, sent by the King no less, and I am looking for a Brave Knight to battle some big lizardy things. Any chance you chaps might be sort of interested?'

'How much?' said the first Brave Knight.

'Quite a lot, actually,' said Sir Barkworth. 'In fact, to be honest, incredibly.'

'What?'

'Dangerous. Incredibly dangerous.'

119

'No problem,' said the second Brave Knight. 'Dangerous is my middle name.'

'No it isn't,' said the third Brave Knight. 'It's Kevin.'

'I meant, how much would we get paid?' said the first Brave Knight.

'Ah, well now,' said Sir Barkworth. 'The prize is a jewel beyond price, the hand of the King's sister, Morgan le Fey, in marriage.'

Like everyone in Avalon, the Brave Knights had heard about the legendary beauty of Morgan le Fey. Unfortunately they had also heard about the legendary independence of Morgan le Fey. So they knew there was no way she would marry any of them unless she actually wanted to. The King might be offering her hand, but there was no way he had the power to offer the rest of her to go with it.

'Well, it's like this,' said the first Brave Knight. 'Normally yes. I mean, any one of us, or even all of us, would be only too happy to come to the aid of our glorious King Arthur and have the chance of marrying his beautiful sister, but . . .'

'Master, have you told them that there's a set of

dinner plates depicting famous heroes of Avalon and a lovely tabard as well as the princess?' said Nymrod, omitting to mention the gold that was on offer in case the opportunity came to reward himself with it.

'Oh yes, absolutely, gorgeous stuff,' said Sir Barkworth.

'Well, you do indeed paint a tempting picture,' said the first Brave Knight, with the other three nodding in agreement. 'But I fear we are already on a great quest.'

'Mind you, if you're still stuck when we've finished questing,' said the third Brave Knight, 'do look us up again, by all means.'

'Great quest?' said Sir Barkworth.

'Oh yes, extremely great,' said the fourth Brave Knight, 'and unfortunately also top secret.'

'Rightio, jolly good,' said Sir Barkworth.

'But I say, old chip,' said the first Brave Knight, 'there is something you could do for us before you go, if you wouldn't mind.'

'Indeed, old chap, just name it.'

'Just give my toenails a quick trim, would you?' said the Brave Knight, pulling off his boots.

The next morning, with his trusty squire by his side, Sir Barkworth set off, not surprisingly in the wrong direction. Because he had a bit of toenail clipping in his left eye, which forced him to keep it closed, he rode in circles all day until, as night fell, they came to an inn.

'This looks like a nice place,' said Sir Barkworth.

'It is indeed, my lord,' said Nymrod.

'Oh, you have stayed here before?'

'Indeed, my lord, and so did you, last night.'

'Ah. Well, yes, it is a nice place and we will stay here tonight as well.'

To make sure he wouldn't make the same mistake again, the next morning Sir Barkworth closed his left eye and set off in the opposite direction. And it worked. After a long day's ride they reached a magnificent castle.

'I say, Nymrod, that's a magnificent castle,' said Sir Barkworth.

'Indeed, my lord.'

'Methinks it may be paradise,' said Sir Barkworth. 'For I have seen it in my dreams.'

'In your dreams, sire?'

'Absolutely, for how else could I have seen it?'

'It is Camelot, my lord,' said Nymrod.

'Really? I never knew there were two castles with that name.'

'There aren't, my lord.'

And so it was that the first Royal Messenger failed in his quest, though having managed to have such a long conversation without falling off his horses did prove his motor skills were getting better every day.

Queen Igraine,
the Lady of
Vegetables and
Patron Saint of
Organic Radishes.

When Arthur became King, he did indeed banish his mother to the Island of Shallot, which he renamed the Island of Vegetables as he had promised. King Arthur then told Merlin to search the castle for the ugliest, smelliest old crone he could find and that she was to be sent to the Island of Vegetables as Igraine's servant.

Sewyr lived in a crack in the wall of Camelot's main sewer. Her family had lived there for seventeen generations, since they had been granted the right to do so by one of Arthur's ancestors. Sewyr had been named in honour of her home. Now that the drains were blocked and overflowing, her family had been forced to move out and had taken up temporary residence in a broken gristle storage bin in the castle tip. All except Sewyr's grandfather, who said he was too old for change and instead stayed in the drain, coming up for air every fifteen minutes.

Merlin had held auditions and Sewyr had stood out as the winner. She had out-smelled and out-uglied all the others. The fact that she still had

one tooth had gone against her, but it was a lovely shade of green and the frothy dribble that came out of her nose every time she spoke had won the day. She had been put into a big sack and ferried across to the Island of Vegetables.

To call it an island was to flatter it. The Island of Vegetables was little more than a rock shaped, remarkably, like a big potato. To call the castle on it a castle was to flatter it too. It was more like a garden shed with a couple of half-hearted towers, seven windows and a mould-covered door that had once been the side of a cattle stall on Noah's Ark.

'I'll teach the Queen to be such a horrid mummy,' Arthur said. 'Let her eat nothing but gruel with a goat's hoof in it, and use the same hoof I had to use for all those years. And let her eat the gruel from a really rough wooden bowl that has been eaten away by so many woodworms that she only has five minutes before the gruel leaks out all over the table and let her spoon be made of rusty iron with sharp bits and, and . . .'

'Sire, surely you would not punish the lady who gave you life with such cruelty?' said Merlin.

126

'Oh, all right,' said Arthur. 'Don't give her a rusty spoon. Give her a piece of the finest silver cutlery for her watery gruel.'

'Indeed, sire.'

'But make it a fork.'

'Sire, there are many at court who would say your mother has a heart of gold.'

'Yes, her heart is gold like a hard-boiled egg,' said Arthur. 'Dry with the texture of sawdust.'

Merlin knew there was no changing the boy's mind and if he was honest with himself, he hated the old Queen too.

'But to show that I am not totally heartless,' Arthur added, 'we shall give my mother a servant who reflects her importance as the mother of the King.'

'So I should send Sewyr back to her drain?' said Merlin.

'Not likely,' said Arthur. 'No, we shall give her an important title. We hereby name her Lady Sewyr of the Slime.'

'Your majesty's generosity,' said Merlin in a sarcastic voice that went completely over the King's

head, 'is only exceeded by your personal kindness.'

'Maybe you're right,' said Arthur. 'Maybe I'm being too nice. I know niceness is one of my weaknesses. I think that is why my subjects love me so much.'

Change love to loathe and you're absolutely right, thought Merlin.

'Oh, woe is me,' Queen Igraine cried. 'That I should end my life so. After all I did for that ungrateful boy.'

'Maybe, my lady,' Lady Sewyr of the Slime dribbled, 'if you were to write down all the things you did for your son and send it to him, he might change his mind.'

'It's worth a try, I suppose,' said the Queen. 'Bring me paper and a quill that I may write.'

'Paper?'

The only paper Sewyr knew had fallen out of the holes above her head in the drains. It had been

soft and crumpled with perforations and full of extreme unpleasantness.

'Umm, well now. I'll see what I can find,' said Sewyr and went off to rummage through the castle cupboards.

There were only two cupboards as it was a very small castle. One was full of dried gruel and the other was empty apart from a goat's hoof. Nor was there any wallpaper in any of the rooms, but for all her grossness, Sewyr was a resourceful person. She went down to the kitchen and got a sharp knife.

'As you know, your son forbade you writing materials so this is all I can find, my lady,' she said, handing Igraine a square of grey material.

'It's hairy,' said Igraine. 'Is that the best you can do?'

'It is, my lady.'

'What is it? I mean, where did you get it?'

'It is skin, from my back, my lady, and I brought you some ink and a nib,' said Sewyr.

'Red ink? It's not a very friendly colour, is it?'

'Sorry, my lady, but that is the colour my blood is.'

129

'And the nib?'

'I had no need of that toenail,' Sewyr whimpered. 'Would you excuse me, my lady? I must go up to the roof and scream in agony for a while.'

'Yes, yes, off you go,' said Igraine, 'but do try to scream quietly. I am trying to concentrate on a letter to my son, you know.'

'Thank you, my lady,' Sewyr cried and left the room.

As luck would have it, Sewyr's screaming was no distraction at all. The old servant had gone no more than ten steps from her mistress's door when she fainted. By the time she came to, several hours later, the Queen had finished her letter and was calling for her dinner.

'Just give me a few minutes, my lady,' Sewyr cried and crawled off towards the kitchen.

'Well, hurry up, I'm hungry,' shouted the Queen after her. 'And make sure you wash the goat's hoof properly, it was covered in hair and cobwebs last time.'

'Yes, my lady.'

Even I, who am the humblest of the humble,

should not be treated this way, Sewyr whispered inside her head. She decided to flee the Island of Vegetables at the earliest opportunity. She spat into Igraine's gruel and carried the bowl up to her mistress.

'I'm not sure if I am just forgetting how wonderful proper food is, or if I am, heaven forbid, actually learning to love gruel,' said the Queen, 'but it actually tastes better than usual.'

'That'll be the secret ingredient, my lady,' said Sewyr.

'Secret ingredient?' asked the Queen. 'What secret ingredient?'

'Can't say, my lady. If I did, it wouldn't be secret and it would lose its magic,' said Sewyr.

She may have been filthy, a peculiar shape and covered in scabs, which were another of her secret ingredients, but Sewyr was not stupid. *If I was,* she thought, *I would consider it an honour to serve a queen.*

She thought back to the crack in the sewer wall that had been her home for so many years, and it didn't seem so bad after all. At least there, no one had taken the skin off her back or made her clean under their toenails with her teeth. At least there she had

people who loved her – not much, admittedly, but enough to apologise after they had kicked her. Back then she had been sick of her home. Now she was homesick.

And of course, there was Gerald. For years Gerald had begged for her hand in marriage, and not just her hand, in fact, but all of her. She had spurned him, selfishly thinking she could do better than a husband with only one eye, and more warts than a giant warty toad. But now, as she curled up in her bucket and tried to sleep, she realised that love was more important than looks and Gerald certainly loved her with all his heart. Not just his heart, too, but his liver and kidneys and even his strange left foot shaped like the hoof she put in her mistress's gruel each night.

'Oh Gerald,' she cried out, 'how could I have been so blind?'

'Shut up,' the Queen called down from above. 'I'm trying to sleep.'

'Here is my letter to the King,' said Igraine the next morning. 'How are we to get it to him?'

'There is only one visitor to our island, and he comes but once a month, my lady,' said Sewyr. 'It is the Gruel Delivery Man in his coracle.'

'Can he be trusted?'

'That I cannot say, my lady,' said Sewyr, seeing an opportunity opening up. 'Perhaps I should go in person and make sure your precious letter reaches the King.'

'I'm not sure that's such a good idea,' said the Queen. 'How can I be certain you will return?'

Oh deary me, thought Sewyr, *not quite as stupid as you look.*

'But my lady, how would anyone in their right mind prefer living in a smelly drain over serving a great queen?'

The Queen was not as clever as she looked either and when Sewyr told her that the Gruel Delivery Man was Sewyr's own twin brother and that he would be happy to stay and look after the Queen while Sewyr was away, that seemed to allay her suspicions.

'Besides, my lady,' Sewyr continued, 'the coracle

133

is only large enough for one person, so if I am to go to Camelot, then he must stay here until I return.'

'All right,' said the Queen, 'but if you fail to deliver my letter and secure my release, I shall put the Curse of the Bagpipes on you.'

The Curse of the Bagpipes was one of the worst curses known to medieval man. For seven days and nights the victim could hear nothing but the awful noise of bagpipes inside their head. It was so loud that it drowned out every other sound. On the eighth day, the bagpipes themselves tracked the victim down and kicked them to death. Only one curse was worse and that was the Curse of the Endless Bagpipes, where they didn't kick you to death, but just kept wailing for ever and ever until you died screaming or actually started to like their awful noise. If that did happen then they stopped playing immediately. It was a very powerful curse and it could tell if you were just pretending to like their wailing.[41]

---

[41] *In 1562 bagpipes were declared illegal in most civilised countries and remained so until Queen Victoria, who was as mad as a hyperactive puppy, repealed the law in Britain. Since then bagpipes have been used as an instrument of torture by many evil dictators.*

134

At the end of the week the Gruel Delivery Man arrived. Before the Queen could speak to him, Sewyr whisked him down to the kitchen.

'If you will pretend you are my twin brother, Tyrd, and do as I ask, I shall be forever in your debt,' she said.

'But I am your twin brother, Tyrd,' said Tyrd. 'Do you not recognise me?'

'Oh,' said Sewyr. 'Of course I don't recognise you. We lived in almost total darkness in the sewers, remember, not to mention being covered from head to foot in unmentionable stuff. Half the time, I couldn't even recognise our own mother. You've no idea how many times I cried myself to sleep thinking my mother had thrown me into the sewage, only to find out later it had been a complete stranger I had been trying to snuggle up to.'

'You too, eh?' said Tyrd.

'Mind you,' said Sewyr, 'now I look at you, I can see we're identical.'

'Well, not completely,' said Tyrd. 'I mean, I'm a man and you're a woman. You are a woman, aren't you?'

'I think so.'

Not realising that Sewyr had no intention of returning, Tyrd agreed to take her place while she delivered the Queen's letter.

As she paddled the coracle back to the castle, Sewyr slid her fingernail under the Queen's seal and opened the letter.

But I am your mother, already.
Go ahead and break my heart
after all I've done for you.
Three weeks I was in labour.
You ruined my figure,
and this is all the thanks I get.

'I think I'm on the King's side,' Sewyr muttered and threw the letter into the lake, where it drifted down to lie on a bed of soft mud and wait for the years to pass until a fictional creature called Gollum would find it and use it to wrap up a Very Important Ring he had found.

As Sewyr had pointed out, her family lived in almost total darkness and were usually covered from

head to foot in unpleasantness. So when she got back to Camelot, she sank the coracle by cutting a big gash in it, rubbed herself in dirt, started talking in a deep voice and pretended she was her twin brother. This meant that one month later when Tyrd would have loaded up his coracle and carried the next month's supply of dried gruel over to the Island of Vegetables, no one did. This meant that Tyrd and the Queen had nothing to eat and because no contact with Camelot was allowed, no one realised. So Tyrd and the Queen starved to death.[42]

Meanwhile, Sewyr revealed her true identity to Gerald, who fainted fifteen times until she stopped revealing herself. He then declared his undead love[43] for her and she agreed to marry him. They moved into a delightful home under a wet rock and lived happily ever after, surrounded by seventeen gorgeously malformed one-eyed children and a pet rabbit called Lovely.

---

[42] *What really happened was that the Queen ate Tyrd and then died of food poisoning.*

[43] *Which is a bit like undying love only with pimples and open sores.*

Lord Pleat of Perivale's journey to Wales, avoiding the Valley of Tears but landing in the Ditch of Sniffles.

Lord Pleat of Perivale was the most reluctant of the Royal Messengers. He was so afraid of travelling – in fact, so afraid of everything – that in order to take as long as possible reaching Wales, Lord Pleat paid someone to steal his horse and got his very helpful squire to drop a very heavy rock on Lord Pleat's right foot. He then dropped an even heavier rock on his very helpful squire. The result was that he had a serious limp and his very helpful squire became less helpful, extremely flat and quite a lot dead.

Hopefully, he thought as he hopped down the road into the darkness, *dragons will be extinct before I reach the Welsh border, or at the very least someone else will have found a Brave Knight.*

What he didn't take into account was that every single passing idiot with a horse and cart would insist on giving him a lift.

'Excuse me, my lord,' they would say as they drew alongside the hopping lord, 'I can't help noticing that you've got a bad foot.'

'Indeed.'

'So, noble lord,' the idiot would continue, 'I would consider it a great prilivij, privylodge, um, honour, if you'm would allow me to render you some assisstun, assytunce, some help and give you a lift.'

The idiot would then make his family lie in the back of the cart on top of the cow dung to make a comfortable bed for Lord Pleat to sit on.

'No, no, my good man, it's fine, thank you,' Lord Pleat would reply. 'It's such a nice day I thought I would take a walk.'

'You bain't walking. You'm 'oppin'.'

'No, I'm fine, thank you.'

'And it bain't a nice day. It be raining cats and them other things.'

'Potatoes,' the idiot's wife would shout from her bed of dung.

'Dogs,' the children would cry.

And the more he insisted he didn't want a lift, the more the idiots thought he did. They picked him up and chucked him in the back of the cart, often missing the human cushions. Quite often these lifts only lasted a few minutes because in the Dark Ages it was against the law for peasants to travel more than

two kilometres from their homes. After he had been chucked into the back of fifteen different carts, Lord Pleat just threw himself into a ditch as soon as he saw or heard anyone coming, which at least washed most of the cow dung off him, though he did keep finding fish in his pockets.

As Lord Pleat lay on his back in the ditch, staring up at the stars in the night sky, they began to fall on him. He was about to cry out when he realised there was no night sky and the stars that were falling were very big snowflakes that soon buried him.

'Excuse me,' said a voice. 'Are you going to keep lying on me indefinitely or are you going to move?'

There was someone lying in the ditch beneath him. That would explain the strange warmth he felt in his back.

'And another thing,' said the voice. 'This is my ditch and I don't remember inviting you to share it with me.'

Lord Pleat tried to sit up. But the sheer weight of the snow on top of him pinned him down.

'Can't move,' he said. 'Sorry.'

The person underneath wriggled out and sat

up. It was not, as Lord Pleat had assumed, a smelly old tramp, but a woman who wasn't old or even, considering where she had been lying, that smelly. The woman scraped at the snow until the two of them were sitting facing each other in a sort of igloo.

Ever since he had been born, Lord Pleat of Perivale had been so nervous of women that he had even been shy of his own mother. When he became a teenager it had got even worse. If a pretty girl came within a hundred metres of him, he blushed bright red and began to sweat. It was so bad that he had even thought of becoming a monk so he could go away to a closed monastery where no woman would ever set foot. He would have done so, too, but he had a terrible allergy to religion.

And now here he was closer to a female lady woman person than he had ever been, apart from his own mother, and she was smiling at him, which his mother had never done, and she was taking a handkerchief and wiping the mud away from his face.

He felt himself going faint. Then he stopped feeling faint because he had fainted. It was even worse

when he woke up. He was lying on his back with his head in the female lady woman person's lap and she was stroking his forehead with some wet leaves.

This made him stop being awake because he had fainted again. This happened quite a lot of times until finally he managed to stay awake by staring at a lump of snow above him and pretending it was a cloud.

'Fear not, my lord,' said the female lady woman person, 'for I mean you no harm.'

Lord Pleat tried to speak, but no words came out.

'These leaves,' the lady said as she continued to wipe them across his forehead, 'are the soothing balm of bladderwrack and purslane and shall calm thy nerves.'

And it worked. Lord Pleat of Perivale felt the fear he had known all his life gradually fade until he was no longer terrified of being so close to a female lady woman person. He found himself not only relaxing, but actually enjoying lying there with his head in her lap.

'Who are you?' he said.

'I am Verdygrys, the Lady of the Ditch,' said the woman.

'Surely you mean the Lady of the Lake?' said Lord Pleat.

'Sadly no,' said Verdygrys. 'I was up for that job, but my rival placed me under a curse that doomed me to forever live in this ditch far from home and the land I love.'

Lord Pleat of Perivale felt his heart twitter. Not only had this beautiful enchantress charmed away his shyness, she had even filled him with thoughts of love and the incredible idea that he might not have to spend the rest of his life on his own with nothing but his collection of home-made cardboard castles and interesting feathers.

'There is no curse that cannot be lifted,' he said, blushing bright red, 'by love.'

'My lord,' said Verdygrys, melting into his arms.

And as they kissed the snow melted too, the ditch dried up and the sun came out, which was very strange as it was the middle of the night.

In the Middle Ages, which were also called the Dark Ages, especially at night-time, there was a very

good law which said that no matter what you were doing and who you were doing it for, even the King, if you met your one true love (as long as they weren't from Wales[44]), you could stop doing whatever it was and go home and live happily ever after.

It turned out that Verdygrys was actually Lady Verdygrys of Aquitaine, which was a bit of France, but Lord Pleat of Perivale was in love and prepared to forgive his wife for being anything, even French.

So Lord Pleat of Perivale and Lady Verdygrys of Aquitaine knocked two passing peasants off their horses, which lords were not only allowed but even encouraged to do, mounted up and rode back to Camelot, where they were married and lived happily ever after, except for the bits when they weren't happy, which everyone has. They had seventeen children, which meant most of the time they were far too tired to live happily or unhappily ever after as all they really wanted to do was go to sleep unconsciously ever after.

---

[44]   *TRUE HISTORICAL FACT: In the Middle Ages it was against the law for anyone from England to marry a Welsh person.*

145

Learning to fly after learning not to cry when you crash into the ground, big trees, assorted rocks and the occasional relative.

It's hard to imagine that something as big and ungainly as a dragon can fly. All dragons have fat bottoms and short legs so running along like a bird and soaring up into the sky does not come easily to them. Even most young dragons find it hard to imagine they will ever be able to fly.

It's traditional for the father to teach his children flying, while the mother handles the cooking – roasting small animals without frying them to a crisp or getting their hooves stuck up your nose, how to make a delicious pour-over sauce from simple insects, and managing it all without thumbs.

So it was that when Bloat was ten years old, Spikeweed took him to the edge of an extremely tall cliff for his first flying lesson.

'I'm scared, Dad,' said Bloat.

'So was I,' said Spikeweed. 'It's only natural, son, but believe me, once you've learnt, you'll wonder how you enjoyed life before. Flying is the most exciting thing you can do. It's what us dragons are all about. Just imagine swooping down out of a cloud,

both nostrils blazing fifty-foot flames as a group of terrified pathetic humans run for cover.'

'I suppose,' said Bloat, trying not to look over the edge.

'No doubt about it, son,' said Spikeweed. 'Idiot humans thinking they'll be safe under a big tree, thinking their stupid thumbs will save them. There's nothing like it.'

'But shouldn't we all try to live together in peace and harmony?' said Bloat, who had been thinking about writing poetry and wondering how he could do it without thumbs.

'Roarin' hippy!' said Spikeweed and pushed his son off the cliff.

'A h h h h h . . . help!'

Bloat realised very, very quickly that noises coming out of his mouth were not going to help him and as he rolled over and over he looked up and realised his dad wasn't going to help him either. So he began flapping his wings as hard as he could and slowly the ground that had been coming towards

him in a very fast blur began to come into focus and slow down. He would have preferred it to slow down a lot more before he hit it, but he ran out of time.

'Not bad, my boy,' said Spikeweed, landing beside him. 'For a first attempt it was actually pretty good. Only one shattered ankle unless I'm mistaken. That'll soon heal. Why, my first time I killed my Auntie Maud, but then if I hadn't landed on her I suppose I'd have broken more than my kneecaps.'

Bloat lay whimpering quietly to himself until night fell and brought rain. He dragged himself back to the cave and tucked his sore leg under his old great-granny.

But like many things in life, the more you do them, the easier they get. The next time his dad threw him off the cliff, Bloat glided towards the ground like a sack of bricks. The first time he had gone down like a sack with a hundred bricks in it. This time there were twenty and he only broke one of his claws.

The third time there were only three bricks in the sack and he didn't even get a bruise because he landed on Gorella, who had been making one of her rare excursions outside.

149

After that Bloat threw himself off the cliff without waiting for his dad to do it, and within six months he had even learned how to take off by running along the ground and waving his wings.

When Bloat had fallen on her, Gorella had undergone a strange transformation. Instead of talking to the stain on the cave wall she thought was her dead husband, she thought she was a geography teacher and began swearing at the wall for not doing its homework on the river systems of Brazil. This was more than strange because geography would not be invented for several hundred years.

Bloat's sister, Depressyng, took to flying like a duck takes to water, though at first it was like a roast duck in apple and mushroom sauce. But she was smaller and lighter than her brother so she got fewer broken bones and bruises, and soon the two young dragons were soaring through the skies, dropping unmentionable things on terrified travellers and dribbling down the chimneys of peasants' cottages into the cauldrons of soup they had roasting on their fires.

HOW TO TALK LIKE AN UPPER-CLASS TWIT

ENGLISH	TWITSPEAK
Oh	Air
I	One
One	One
Five	Fave
Very	Orflee
My	May
Coke	Cake
Cake	Gatoh
G'day	Hair-lair
A pretty girl	Damn fine filly
Oi, mate	I say, old chip
John Smith	The Honourable St.John* Smythe-Smythe
My car	The old bus
My wife	The old gel

*Don't forget that St.John is actually pronounced Sinjun. Ridiculous, isn't it?

Sir Lamorak's journey to The North and Beyond and a Little Bit More.

Sir Lamorak was the only one of the four messengers who was really keen on the mission. He couldn't wait to get going and was determined to be the one who found the Brave Knight. It wasn't the wonderful dinner plates or the tabard, but the glory that it would bring and all the new girlfriends it was sure to get him.

When the Royal Messengers reached the mainland, Sir Lamorak took a quick look at his compass and raced North. As night fell, he continued to ride and as dawn arrived, he was still riding. He put his horse on automatic while he took power naps, and for food he plucked skylarks out of the air. For drink, he opened his mouth as he rode through a ferocious storm. Only when his horse collapsed with exhaustion did he stop. Then he stole a fresh horse from the nearest field and set off again at top speed.

For five days and nights he rode on. He reached The North, but still he did not stop. He left the borders of Avalon behind and rode on into Scotland. The snow, which grew forever deeper, did not slow him down and neither did the ferocious cold. He did not even stop to go to the toilet.

On the seventh minute of the seventh hour of the seventh day on his seventh horse, he finally reached the very northernmost tip of the country and *fell off.*

The Great Roundish Table of the Great Knights of Camelot, who were great, but not as great as King Arthur.

To distract everyone from the smelly drain problem, Merlin suggested to the King that he should order the making of a Great Round Table where all the Knights of Camelot could sit and feast without anyone feeling more important than anyone else.

'But I am more important than anyone else,' said Arthur. 'So where shall I sit?'

'Sire, everyone knows that you are the most important person in creation,' lied Merlin, 'and they all love you for it, but the Great Round Table would only serve to enhance your popularity and unquestioned wonderfulness.'

'I don't see how,' said the King. 'If there isn't a seat that's more important than the rest of them, where shall I sit?'

'Sire, surely you must realise that something as humble as a seat would have no effect on your greatness,' said Merlin. 'No, your majesty, by sitting as an equal with your knights – and of course we all know that you are far, far above them in every way – you will show your people that for all your greatness,

you are also a caring, humble person.'

'Is that good?' said Arthur. 'I mean, being humble and caring doesn't seem so great to me.'

'I promise you, sire, it will make the people love you even more,' said Merlin.

'Is that possible?'

'There is always room for more love, your majesty,' said Merlin. *It certainly couldn't make them love you any less,* he thought.

'Oh, very well, then. Order the Castle Cabinet-maker to build a really big shiny round table and tell him to make sure that it is bigger and shinier and rounder than any other round table ever built,' said the King.

'Indeed, sire, I shall go to him immediately,' said Merlin, rushing out of the room before he threw up. *I don't know how much more of this dreadful little brat I can take,* he thought.

So the Great Round Table was ordered.

Chisyl, the Castle Cabinet-maker, scoured the land for the finest timber, a rafter from a famous theatre, a drawbridge from a great castle, seven ancient oaks from the forests of Savernake and, for

the pegs to hold all the pieces together, he took the wooden leg from Bluebeard the Pirate. Such a table would take at least two years to plane and cut and join and carve before it was finished, so Merlin assisted Chisyl and his carpenters with a few well-chosen bits of magic and a week later it was finished.

The Great Round Table was assembled in the mighty dining hall of Camelot by the fifteen Table Carriers, who had to take the doors of the dining hall off to even get it into the room. And on the eighth day, before all the assembled important people of Camelot, King Arthur unveiled it.

'This is the greatest, most beautiful, most perfect table ever and it was designed by me,' said the King.

The Table Unveilers – three beautiful maidens, semi-finalists from *Avalon's Got Talent* who had been trained especially for the purpose – pulled the dazzling sheet away and the assembled gathering cheered.

All except the King. He walked round the table thirteen times and then stamped his feet, making the bells on the end of his slippers tinkle.

'I said a round table!' he screamed.

'It is round, sire,' said Chisyl

'No it's not,' said the King. 'There's a huge bump. Look.'

'I realise that your majesty has royal eyes that see far better than those of a humble cabinet-maker,' said Chisyl, running his hand along the table's edge, 'but I can feel no bump.'

'Are you blind, man?'

'I am, sire,' said Chisyl.

'Ah,' said the King. 'In that case we have a problem. As the King I cannot touch a lowly carpenter. Otherwise I could take your hand and put it on the bump.'

'Might I make a suggestion, sire?' said Merlin.

'I don't know,' said the King. 'Might you?'

'Yes, sire.'

'Very well, then, you have my permission to suggest.'

'Well, sire, am I not the Top Wizard of Avalon?'

'Indeed,' said Arthur. 'Apart from me, of course.'

'Yes, um, exactly, sire,' said Merlin. 'So you, the King, as the, er, topmost wizard of all wizards, could take my hand, could you not?'

'Where?'

'Sire?'

'Take your hand where?' said the King.

'No, no, sire. I meant, you could take my hand in your hand,' said Merlin, 'then you could show me the bump. Then I could take the carpenter's hand and show him the bump.'

'You would do that for me?' said Arthur. 'You would touch a peasant?'

'I would, sire,' said Merlin.

'You are a true and wonderful servant,' said Arthur. 'Here, have another knighthood.'

'You are too kind, sire.'

'Oh, am I? You think I should keep the knighthood?'

'Oh no, sire,' said Merlin, well aware that each one of the forty-seven knighthoods the King had given him carried an income of fifteen shillings and three pence a year.

Arthur put on a silk glove, took Merlin's hand in his and led him over to the table.

'See, it's obvious, isn't it?' he said.

'Sire, it may be obvious to one as sensitive as

you, but to a mere mortal like myself, I cannot feel the deformity,' said Merlin.

'But it stands out a mile,' said Arthur. 'Oh, no, hold on, I put your hand in the wrong place. Now can you feel it?'

Merlin shook his head. This happened three more times until the wizard lied and agreed that there was indeed an imperfection.

'I think, sire,' he said, 'that we should mark it with a piece of chalk so that less sensitive beings than yourself can find it.'

Merlin then took Chisyl's hand and led him over to the table. As he did so, he spelled out with his finger in the carpenter's hand: *I know the table is perfectly round. You know the table is perfectly round. We both know the famous King Arthur is an idiot, but he's the King and he has several executioners with very big axes. And remember, these are dangerous times. Repeat this to anyone and I will kill you.*

'What are you writing in the peasant's hand?' said the King.

'He was writing, sire? I am but an ignorant peasant and cannot read,' Chisyl lied.

'Are you sure?' said the King.

'Oh yes, sire,' said Chisyl. 'My hand was itching and the noble Merlin was scratching it for me.'

'True, your highness,' said Merlin. 'The lower classes itch a lot.'

'Do they really?' said the King. 'How fascinating. So Mother was right, the peasants are like mangy dogs.'

'Oh yes, sire,' said Chisyl. 'Mange is an old tradition in my family.'

At this the King jumped on a chair and began waving a lavender-scented handkerchief in the air, but he calmed down when Merlin assured him that only the lower classes could catch it.

'Now see here, my man,' said Merlin, guiding Chisyl's hand round the outside of the Great Round Table. 'Surely you can feel the bump now.'

'Oh yes, master,' said Chisyl. 'How could I have missed it?'

'Exactly,' said the King. 'But I am a wise and just King so I will overlook it this time.'

'The bump?' said Chisyl.

'No, you low creature,' said the King. 'I will

overlook your missing such an obvious fault in this exquisite table, a table that all shall know was designed by me, King Arthur, the greatest table-designing King who has ever lived.'

'Indeed, sire,' said Merlin.

So the fifteen Table Carriers were summoned. The two doors were taken off their hinges and the Great Round Table was carried back to Chisyl's workshop. As the table was already perfect, it occurred to the cabinet-maker to simply pretend he'd done something and send it back, but he made it a bit smaller in case the King realised it hadn't been touched.

The next day the table was brought back and once again King Arthur insisted there was still a bump on it.

'But it's in a different place,' he said. 'You are a fool. You have removed one bump, but in doing so you have created another.'

So the fifteen Table Carriers were summoned. The two doors were taken off their hinges again and the Great Round Table was carried back to Chisyl's workshop in the special cart towed by four great elephants.

The next day the table was brought back and this time King Arthur insisted there were two bumps.

And so it went on.

And on.

And on, until:

'Finally,' said the King. 'It is as perfect as I am. At last I have a table that is fine enough for me to sit at. Bring me a bowl of pheasant soup that I may be the first to eat off my wonderful Great Round Table.'

'But, your majesty . . .' Merlin began. The King waved him away and called for his soup.

The soup arrived and the serving wench placed the perfectly round china bowl on the perfectly round Great Round Table, where it promptly fell straight into the King's perfectly placed lap.

Screaming in pain was followed by screaming in anger, which was followed by more screaming in anger because all the baths were full of disgusting fifteenth-hand bath water because of the blocked drains, which was followed by huge amounts of swearing as Nana Agnys was summoned and took the King up to the roof to get washed off in the rain, which wasn't so much rain as very cold driving snow.

The Great Round Table, which had always been perfectly round from the first day it was created, had been planed and shaved so much that it was now the Great Round Stick. It had been cut down so much that it was pushed quietly into the corner and renamed the Great Round Pepper Pot Stand. It had ended up so small there was not even room to stand the salt next to the pepper.

Once again Merlin saved the day. A few quick spells to wipe the whole fiasco from the young King's mind, followed by another to recreate the original Great Round Table, put things right. Although Arthur kept wondering why he had burnt legs.

'If I didn't know better,' he said to Nana Agnys, 'I'd swear someone had tipped hot soup in my lap.'

'Oh, you and your vivid imagination,' said Nana Agnys.

As King Arthur's nanny, she was bound to love and protect her young charge, but she wasn't blind and was only too aware what a revolting little child he was. Like Merlin, she was growing more and more convinced that Arthur was not the great King Uther-Pendragon's son. The boy did not have one

saving grace, apart from his lovely legs and mauve tights, of course. There was not one trait of his father's quick-witted and fearless character, nor anything of his mother's cold determination.

Maybe, thought Nana Agnys, *I should try to discover the truth.*

Maybe, thought Merlin, *I should try to find out who stole the true King and put this idiot in his place.*

And why, they both thought.

Or not, they also thought, deciding that maybe an easy life with no complications was the way to go.

Sir Bedivere's journey to The West – land of opportunity and very rich, handsome and gullible knights.

The fourth Royal Messenger, Sir Bedivere, had actually been away from Camelot on many occasions. Each time he had slipped away under cover of darkness and avoided the castle gatekeepers by using a small boat he kept hidden under a bush at the back of the castle. His 'little holidays', as he called them, always had one very simple aim. To transform other people's gold and jewels into his gold and jewels. Because of his totally unscrupulous nature, he had become the richest person in Camelot.

So if all else fails, he thought, *I can always bribe someone to take on the dragons,* though parting with any of his money would most certainly be the very last resort as it always gave him an upset stomach.

'I haven't got where I am today by giving money away,' he said.

'Indeed, master,' said his squire, Barnakle, who had not been paid a single groat in the past year.

This was exactly how long he had been Sir Bedivere's squire and in that time his master had borrowed everything his servant owned, including

his socks. This was the Olde English meaning of the word 'borrow', which means 'take and not give back, ever'.

There had only been one occasion when Sir Bedivere had returned something after he had borrowed it from Barnakle. It was a sticking plaster that he had worn on a very nasty pimple for seven weeks, though he borrowed it again a few months later before handing it back for good, by which time it had lost all its sticking ability and it was impossible to tell which side was which.

'Thank you, my lord,' Barnakle had said as he scraped the residue off.

Sir Bedivere was not stupid. Other things he was not included nice, popular, conscientious, hard-working and honest. He was probably the nastiest of the Knights of Camelot and therefore the most likely to lure an unsuspecting knight back to venture into the dragon's cave, except to do so would require quite a bit of effort, something Sir Bedivere was not fond of.

Once they had left the valley a few hours behind them, Sir Bedivere left the main road and travelled

along a pleasant lane until they were out of sight of everything, except the bushes on each side of them, four sparrows and a dragonfly.

'Right,' he said, pulling out a scroll. 'Let's have a look.'

'At what, my lord?' said Barnakle. 'All I can see are some bushes and four sparrows. There was a dragonfly, but it's just flown off.'

'Not that, you idiot,' said Sir Bedivere. 'My hostel guide. I'm looking for a nice remote inn where we can go and take our ease for a couple of weeks while the other idiots rush round looking for a knight.'

He may have been tighter than a baby mosquito's left ear, but life with Sir Bedivere was a lot more relaxed than it was with any other knight. Although he had never been paid, Barnakle was envied by all the other squires, who spent all day rushing round and all night polishing armour.

'This looks like the perfect place,' said Sir Bedivere, pointing to the scroll. 'The Owl and The Cauliflower. It is seventeen miles from any other building, hidden in the middle of a thick forest and,

as luck would have it, is fifteen miles along this very track.'

'Excellent, my lord,' said Barnakle, well aware that the next few weeks would be ones of pleasant luxury followed by a very rapid running away in the middle of the night to avoid paying the bill.

Still, he thought, *it's nothing we haven't done before.*

'Indeed, master, I packed the Cloaks of Invisibility just in case,' he added.

People like Sir Bedivere, who lie and cheat their way through life, gathering large amounts of money as they go, seldom get what people think they deserve. They steal crown jewels and get away with it. They rob banks and then get paid a reward for false information that gets someone else arrested for it. They run away with other people's wives, sheep and cauliflowers, and instead of being condemned for it, everyone thinks they are exciting and romantic like Robin Hood[45] or Ned Kelly, who were both common criminals with very good public relations.

---

[45] *Which, of course, is where the word 'hood', meaning gangster, comes from.*

170

So it was that when Sir Bedivere arrived at the inn and had booked the finest suite and had a bit of a rest in the huge comfy bed with a glass of champagne and a bowl of chocolate-covered strawberries and then gone downstairs for dinner, the only other guest at the inn turned out to be the Bravest Knight in the Whole World. He was EXACTLY what Sir Bedivere had been sent out to look for.

Tall, dark and handsome yet at the same time of medium height with a head of golden hair and skin like polished porcelain yet at the same time with a hint of a beard that was just enough to show he was a fearless superhero.

Bit too perfect to let him get burnt by a dragon, really, thought Sir Bedivere. *Still, business is business and I can see it now as the King hands me a huge bag of gold sovereigns for being the one to bring back THE Brave Knight to kill the evil dragon.*

'Good Sir Knight,' said Sir Bedivere. 'Well met and with whom do I have the honour of dining?'

'I am Sir Lancelot,' said the Bravest Knight in the Whole World.

'Ah, well, sir, your name is legend,' said Sir

Bedivere, who could flatter the back and front legs off a whole field of donkeys. 'And what brings you to Avalon?'

'I am freshly returned from foreign parts, where I lanced a lot of Heathen Goths and slayed Vlad the Inhaler himself,' said Sir Lancelot.

'Vlad the Inhaler?'

'Yes. He is the son of Vlad the Impaler, who I also lanced a lot, and he has a bad sinus problem,' said Sir Lancelot. 'Or rather, I should say he *had* a bad sinus problem. Breathing no longer causes him any difficulty. And I am here,' Sir Lancelot continued, 'to try and win the hand of the King's sister, Morgan le Fey.'

'Indeed sir, well, I may be able to help you there,' said Sir Bedivere, proving yet again that fortune favours the selfish and greedy.

'You know the lady?'

'Indeed, sir,' lied Sir Bedivere, unless seeing her from a window as she crossed the courtyard qualified as knowing.

'And is her beauty as enchanting as it is said to be?'

'There are not words enough to describe it,' said Sir Bedivere.

'So she's hot stuff then, eh?' said Sir Lancelot.

'My lord, so hot she could boil a kettle if you sat it down on the other side of the room,' said Sir Bedivere. 'And when she sings or simply just speaks, why, nightingales feel so inadequate they beat their heads against trees and are struck dumb.'

'Wow. And you can introduce me to her?' said Sir Lancelot. 'If 'tis so, I should be forever in your debt.'

Not so much forever, thought Sir Bedivere, *only until you have rewarded me with your entire wealth.*

'I think that the Lady Morgan le Fey is away at present,' said Sir Bedivere, who still fancied a week of peace and quiet at the inn sitting in the sunshine listening to the singing of the birds and the clinking of Sir Lancelot's bag of gold, which he had just noticed.

'That is a fine bag, Sir Lancelot,' he said.

'Indeed it is, for it was given to me by none other than Leonardo da Vinci,' said Sir Lancelot. 'He used to keep his pencils in it.'

173

'It must be priceless.'

'Indeed. There are three hundred gold sovereigns inside it, yet I believe the bag itself is worth ten times that amount,' said Sir Lancelot.

'Oh my goodness,' said Sir Bedivere, beginning to dribble uncontrollably.

Barnakle had seen his master drool in the presence of wealth many, many times before and always carried a big hankie for such occasions. With one quick flick of his wrist he cleared his master's chin before Lancelot noticed.

'But see here, my good and helpful friend,' said Sir Lancelot, 'let me make you a present of it. This priceless bag and its contents are mere trifles compared to the treasure of my Lady Morgan le Fey, whose heart I hope to win with your selfless help.'

'Oh, I couldn't,' said Sir Bedivere with all his fingers and toes crossed behind his back.

'I insist,' said Sir Lancelot. 'It is the least I can do.'

Oh wow, there's more? thought Sir Bedivere. The sheer weight of the bag and its gold in his hands made him so weak with delight that he would have

fallen over if Barnakle hadn't propped him up.

Who's the coolest knight in the whole world? he thought. *And who's going to be the richest knight in the whole world and the most popular knight in Camelot?*

Ooh, I wonder who it could be?

Oh, of course, it's moi, the great rich and famous Sir Bedivere of Bedivere.

Yeah, I TOTALLY RULE!

He didn't answer the bit about who was the most popular knight, because he didn't really care about that. As long as he got all the cash, people could dislike him as much as they liked.

'I believe, Sir Lancelot,' he said, 'that the angel of whom we speak is due to return to Camelot in five days' time.'

'Excellent,' said Sir Lancelot. 'We shall rest here until then and feast on the finest venison and wines which it will be my honour and delight to provide you with.'

'As you wish, my lord,' said Sir Bedivere. 'I was on my way to a dark cold monastery to purge my soul in a cold dungeon wearing nothing but a horse-hair shirt and eating naught but gravel for a week,

175

but for you, my lord, I shall sacrifice my penance and be your guest.'

'Wonderful,' said Sir Lancelot. 'You are a good and true friend and I shall give thanks to the gods by throwing a bag of gold down the Well of Thanksgiving at the back of this very inn.'

Sir Bedivere gave a barely discernible nod to Barnakle, who went out to the stables and put on his wellies. It would not be the first time he had gone down a wishing well to relieve it of its contents and no doubt it would not be the last.

IMPORTANT NOTE

The Leonardo da Vinci referred to in this chapter was not THE famous Leonardo da Vinci, the great artist and inventor. Nor was it his even more famous descendant, Leonardo da Vinci, who won the 2007 series of Transylvania Waters's Got Talent with his brilliant song 'I'm In The Mood For Blood'. This was an earlier ancestor called Leonardo da Vinci, who was very famous for his wonderful handbags.

Do YOU HAVE A LAZY KITTEN THAT LIES AROUND ALL DAY AND NEVER TAKES ANY EXERCISE?

THEN YOU NEED DOCTOR MERLIN'S

KITTYLENE TRAMPOLINE

HOURS OF FUN FOR ALL THE FAMILY*

* Well, maybe not so much fun for Kitty. Like I said earlier, don't try this at home.

And then there were twenty-three, hold on, twenty-seven, no, no, wait, thirty-two, there's another one, um, thirty-three, no, thirty-nine, hold on, forty-seven baby dragons.

'**Y**ou know how you keep banging on about being the King of the Dragons?' said Primrose.

'Well, I am. I am Spikeweed, King of the Dragons,' said Spikeweed.

'As you are forever saying,' said Primrose. 'Trouble is, you are also King of the smallest Kingdom of anything, with a total population of five.'

'Hey, it's quality, not quantity, that counts,' said Spikeweed.

'Oh yes, of course, try telling that to those feeble Italian dragons,' said Primrose. 'If they realised there was only five of us, they'd be here tomorrow morning and have us conquered before morning tea.'

'Um, er, not necessarily,' said Spikeweed, but he knew his wife was right. 'And another thing.'

'What?'

'What's tea?'

'Never mind all that,' said Primrose. 'The point I was trying to make is that we need to increase our population.'

'And how are we going to do that?'

'Duh,' said Primrose, pointing up at the three big trees that stood outside the cave.

At the top of each tree was a brand new dragon's nest.

'I've already started,' she continued. 'I'm going to sit on two eggs and the kids are going to sit on the two other nests. If you hadn't burnt down all the other trees we could have hauled your old granny up and sat her on another clutch.'

And then for the first, and probably last, time in his life, Spikeweed had an idea that was not totally useless. It was in fact, a good, though extremely revolutionary, idea.

'Why do we have our eggs in the tops of trees?' he said.

'Well, that's where we build our nests, stupid,' said Primrose.

'Why?'

'So they are safe from predators, of course.'

'What predators?'

'Dinosaurs, of course,' said Primrose.

'You mean all the huge animals that we roasted into extinction?' said Spikeweed.

'Exactly.'

'Extinction? Extinction? Ring a bell?' said Spikeweed. 'So how many dinosaurs are there left?'

'Well, probably, um . . .' Primrose began.

'None.'

'Yes.'

'So we could actually build our nests on the ground?' said Spikeweed.

'Of course not,' said Primrose.

'Why not?'

'Because we build them in the tops of trees.'

'Why?'

'So they are safe from predators, of course.'

'What predators?'

'Dinosaurs,' said Primrose. 'Oh.'

'Yes.'

'Um.'

'And another thing,' said Spikeweed. 'The nest is only there to stop the eggs falling out and if the nest is on the ground, they can't fall out. So we don't actually need to build a nest at all. We could just scrape a little dent in the ground to stop them rolling away.'

'Wow,' said Primrose, seeing her husband in a whole new light, which was hardly surprising because it was dawn and the sun had just come up.

'Here's a thought,' Spikeweed continued. 'Why not just lay some eggs in the back of the cave and while I lift my granny off the ground, you could roll them underneath her.'

Primrose was almost speechless. She was amazed at how she had misjudged her husband. Sure, it had taken his tiny brain about thirty-five years to come up with one good idea, but it was a seriously good idea.

'You really are the King of the Dragons,' she said, fluttering her lovely eyelashes at him.

'I call it Speed-Breeding,' said Spikeweed proudly.

Dragon eggs take anywhere from one week to seventeen years to hatch out depending on the circumstances. Being placed beneath a very old dragon where the temperature was always a constant 51 degrees and the atmosphere a steady 115 per cent moisture content, due to regular leaking, can make a dragon egg hatch out in as few as eight days.

So it was that within one month, Spikeweed was King of a population of twenty-three, no, hold on, twenty-seven, no, wait, thirty-two, no, there's another one . . .

'Can we come down now?' Bloat shouted down from the top of his tree.

'Yes, I'm really, really bored,' shouted Depressyng from the top of hers.

'Me too,' said Primrose.

As the Gorella incubator was doing so well, the three dragons up in the trees pushed their eggs out of their nests and sent them crashing down to the ground, where the thirty-three, no, thirty-nine, hold on, forty-seven baby dragons ate them for breakfast.

Meanwhile, simultaneously, concurrently at the same time as some of that stuff had been happening . . .

Although Lady Petaluna was an honest child, Morgan le Fey found it hard to believe that Romeo Crick really was fireproof. So she decided to go and see for herself. Lady Petaluna had told her that the Cook was extremely protective of the boy, barely letting him out of her sight, so she would have to go in disguise so as not to arouse any suspicion.

'You are quite sure that this is what a common serving wench wears?' said Morgan le Fey as Lady Petaluna tied the last strips of torn rag round her ankle. She had been surrounded by servants her whole life. She knew they spoke funny and had peculiar skin conditions, but she had never paid much attention to their dress code.

'Yes, my lady,' said Lady Petaluna, 'though there is still a problem with your smell.'

'I don't have a smell,' said Morgan le Fey. 'Princesses do not smell.'

'That's the problem. Serving wenches do.'

'Oh, and I suppose I'd be right in thinking it's not a particularly nice smell.'

'That depends who you are and what you compare it to, my lady.'

'Meaning?'

'If you were a flea and you lived on a pig's bottom, you would probably think it was a delicate and rather sweet smell,' said Lady Petaluna.

'And if you were a princess?'

'You might want to throw up a lot.'

Lady Petaluna went off to find a bottle of cabbage water with a dead rat in it. She was right about the throwing-up bit. Morgan le Fey did it a lot.

'Has it got rose petals in it?' she said.

'Yes, my lady. I put them in to make the smell less vomit-making.'

'I hate the smell of roses.'

But even when Lady Petaluna went outside and took the rose petals out of the bottle it didn't really help.

'I'm not sure I can go through with this,' said Morgan le Fey as she barfed for the seventh time. 'If I'm like this now, I can't imagine how I'll feel when you actually open the bottle.'

But Morgan le Fey was not one to give up so she stuffed daisies up each nostril[46] while Lady Petaluna poured the contents of the bottle onto the rags Morgan was wearing.

'OK, let's go,' she said, holding her breath as much as she could.

The dungeons were very close to the kitchens so Morgan le Fey decided they should go there first. If the Cook discovered they had taken Romeo Crick and came after them, the dungeons would be the perfect place to lie low. The Cook would never think to look there.

Morgan le Fey was fascinated by what she saw below stairs. Living in her privileged world she had never seen anything like it.

'Though it is a lot like upstairs, but without daylight or windows or fresh air or cleanliness,' she

---

[46] *Do NOT try this at home and I say this from experience from when my cousin Stephen and I persuaded his younger sister to stuff daisies up her nose. Not only did she do it, but then we got her to stick her finger into a snail's shell and paint her face with it. She had to go to the doctor to get all the daisies taken out and Stephen and I got into Big Trouble, but it was worth it. She was great to play with – we could persuade her to do the grossest things.*

187

said, 'or flowers or birds or smiling or washing.'

Because no one ever went to this part of the castle, she decided it was safe to reveal who she was to Clynk the jailer.

'I guarantee,' Morgan le Fey told Clynk, 'that before the year's end I shall get you and the prisoners set free.'

'Even Lord Resydue the Baby-Eater of Londinium?' said Clynk. 'Surely not him?'

'But if he is left here, then you will have to remain too,' said Morgan le Fey.

'That is true,' said Clynk. 'Unless I use Plan B.'

'Plan B?'

'It is better you do not know what Plan B is, my lady.'

'Fair enough,' said Morgan le Fey. 'Though at a guess I would say it probably involves a certain person changing from a breathing situation to a no-longer-breathing situation.'

'You are as wise as you are beautiful, my lady,' said Clynk.

They left the dungeons and went up the back stairs to the kitchens.

'Everyone is all right except the Cook,' said Lady Petaluna. 'If she asks who you are, tell her you're the new servant girl from the Attic of a Thousand Nanas. She hates the nanas so she never speaks to any of them and would never go up there to check.'

'And if she asks me why I'm here, what should I say?' said Morgan le Fey.

'Tell her you have been sent down to fetch the weekly gristle allowance.'

Of course, the first person they bumped into was the Cook.

'Who are you?' she demanded of Morgan le Fey. 'And what are you doing in my kitchen?'

'If it please you, ma'am,' said Morgan le Fey, curtsying, 'I be Blossom Scroggins, one of the new maids in the Attic of a Thousand Nanas.'

'I hate them nanas,' said the Cook, 'sitting up

189

there in their attic being so high and mighty, while us honest working folk are stuck down here in the steam and the darkness. They should put them down here and give us the bright sunny attics. I mean, all they're doin' is waitin' around to die. They could do that anywhere.'

'Them's exactly the words my mother uses,' said Morgan le Fey. 'She says them nanas is a no-good bunch of scroungers and they should be made to go out and dig for coal, is what she says.'

'Your mother sounds like a smart woman,' said the Cook, putting her arm round Morgan le Fey's shoulder. 'What's a nice girl like you doing working for them useless old biddies?'

''Tis where I was sent, ma'am,' said Morgan le Fey. 'I warn't gived no choice.'

'Maybe I knows your mother,' said the Cook. 'What's her name and what's her occupation?'

'She be called Gladys Scroggins, if it please you, ma'am, and she be a washerwoman,' said Morgan le Fey.

It may seem surprising that, coming from her sheltered background, Morgan le Fey could act so

190

convincingly but, by an amazing piece of good luck, she owned a children's book called *Gladys Scroggins in Wonderland*, which told the story of a washerwoman and her magic bucket. She knew that the Cook would not have read the book, because the lower classes couldn't read on account of it being illegal for them to do so in those days.

'I think I might have met her, you know,' said the Cook. 'Now you be sure to give her my regards when you see her next and here's a nice pig's knuckle for you, my dear.'

'Oh, thank you, ma'am.'

'And you be welcome here whenever you feels like it, my dear,' added the Cook. 'And any time you feel you need to get away from them old biddies upstairs, you just come and see old Cookie.'

'Thank you, ma'am,' said Morgan le Fey. 'Maybe I could get a job down here, helpin's you?'

'That be a great idea,' said the Cook. 'I been thinking I should be getting an apprentice to teach all my recipes to and I think you might be just the girl for the job.'

'I'm sure I should, ma'am. For I do so love

191

the cookin' and potatoes and things like that,' said Morgan le Fey.

'I has a good feelin' about this,' said the Cook.

'So does I,' said Morgan le Fey. *More than you could imagine,* she thought. For not only would she be in the same place as Romeo Crick and so be able to get to know the boy without raising any suspicions, she might even learn how to make beetroot soup and how to get the skin of roast boar as crispy as a winter frost.

'Oh, my lady,' said Lady Petaluna, as soon as they left the kitchens, 'you were brilliant. Why, I almost believed you were Blossom Scroggins myself.'

Every day for the next week Morgan le Fey, disguised as Blossom Scroggins, worked as the Cook's apprentice. On the fifth day the Cook introduced her to Romeo Crick.

'You know,' she said to Morgan le Fey, 'I looks upon young Romeo here as the son I never had and

I'm beginning to look upon you as a daughter.'

'But I already has a mum, ma'am.'

'And brothers and sisters too, no doubt?' said the Cook.

'Yes, ma'am, sixteen of them if it please you,' said Morgan le Fey.

'Sixteen? My goodness me,' said the Cook. 'And here's me with not a one. Now I'm sure your mother wouldn't mind if I took you as my own daughter. I mean, with seventeen of you she probably wouldn't even notice.'

'That be true, ma'am. She can only count up to one.'

'Then it's settled,' said the Cook. 'You shall be my daughter and a big sister to my poor orphaned son Romeo.'

'A sister?' said Romeo. 'I never had one of them, nor a brother, as I can remember.'

'You must have been awful lonely,' said Morgan le Fey.

'Oh no, I had Geoffrey,' said Romeo. 'As good a friend as a boy ever had.'

'And what happened to him then?'

193

'He got struck by lightning,' said Romeo. 'And eated.'

'Eated?' said Morgan le Fey, moving away from the boy. 'Eated? Oh my God. Was you attacked by cannibals?'

'No, no, we all eated him,' said Romeo.

Morgan le Fey moved further away and turned white.

'The crackling was delicious,' said Romeo.

Seeing the expression on Morgan le Fey's face, the Cook explained that Geoffrey was not a small boy, but a large pig.

'So now I has the family I always dreamt of,' the Cook said, putting one arm round Romeo and the other round Morgan le Fey. 'We will celebrate with gristle pie and mulled cabbage water.'

If I had sat down and written a plan, it wouldn't have been any better than this, thought Morgan le Fey.

She soon discovered that what Lady Petaluna had told her about Romeo's amazing abilities was true. She stood open-mouthed as he climbed into the red-hot ovens and scraped them clean. Not only did Romeo Crick glow gold, he was also worth his

weight in it. She had to get him away from the Cook and up into her quarters before her stupid brother found out about him.

It didn't take long for the opportunity to arise. The Cook adored the boy and rarely let him out of her sight, but now she adored Blossom Scroggins too.

Of course, the easiest thing would be to knock the Cook out with a sleeping draught, but the woman was crafty and forever on her guard. She would neither eat nor drink anything that she hadn't prepared herself, yet it seemed she made an exception to that rule whenever Romeo made chocolate truffles for her. It was simple enough to slip something into them as the boy was making them. He was a total innocent and never suspected anyone would do stuff like that. So when Morgan le Fey offered to help him, he was only too happy to let her.

Each night the kitchen staff went back to their hovels, leaving only the Cook, Morgan le Fey and Romeo behind, for their beds were in the kitchen itself. So every night the three of them would eat their dinner at the huge pine table that during the day was the centre of all the cooking activity.

195

And after they had dined on the finest pig's knuckles and fish bladders filled with shredded weasel, they would sit back and relax, and it was then that the Cook would finish her meal off with a few of Romeo's chocolate truffles.

'I do believe, my little angel, that these are the best truffles you have made. They have an almost magical richness to them that almost puts me into a trance,' she said that night.

Then she fell off her chair and lay amongst the straw, snoring like a very large pig with a terrible nasal problem.

'Would you'm like to see outside?' said Morgan le Fey as Blossom,

'What, upstairs?' said Romeo Crick.

'Indeed.'

'It's not allowed. Cook said I was never to go above stairs or something terrible would happen to me and I'd be turned into a carrot.'

''Tain't true,' said Morgan le Fey. 'People can't be turned into carrots. Though I did see someone turned into a potato once, but they got turned back again when the new moon comed.'

196

'But . . .'

'Come on. Old Cookie be fast asleep. We'll be back before she wakes up.'

She took Romeo's hand and led him up the stairs. They passed through the storerooms and up more stairs until they reached ground level, where Lady Petaluna was waiting.

'What're you doing here?' said Romeo Crick.

'You haven't told him yet, then, my lady?' said Lady Petaluna.

'No, I thought I'd wait until we got back to my quarters,' said Morgan le Fey in her proper voice.

'Why are you talking different?' said Romeo, looking frightened. 'I don't want to be here no more. I want to go back down to Cookie.'

Morgan le Fey picked the boy up, slung him over her shoulder and she and Lady Petaluna hurried back along the corridors until they were safely back in the North-West Wing. She sat Romeo Crick down and explained who she was.

'So you're not Blossom Scroggins?' said the boy and, turning to Lady Petaluna, he added, 'And you are not a serving wench?'

'No,' said Morgan le Fey. 'I am Morgan le Fey, the King's sister, and Lady Petaluna is my lady-in-waiting.'

'Oh,' said Romeo Crick a little sadly.

The first time he had set eyes on Lady Petaluna, he had felt a little flutter in his heart. Even with her serving wench disguise and face mask of soot and squashed slugs, she had made his pulses race. Of course, being only eleven, he didn't know why his pulses were racing. He thought it was probably indigestion caused by a particularly delicious lump of gristle, but every time he looked at Petaluna the feeling came back. He had sort of fallen in love with Lady Petaluna, in the only way an eleven-year-old boy can fall in love with an eleven-year-old girl, but now he had discovered she was a lady and not a simple serving wench, he felt his heart sink for he knew she would never be able to love someone as humble as him.

'You deserve better in life than being stuck down in the kitchens with that awful Cook,' said Morgan le Fey.

'But she is like a mother to me,' said Romeo.

'No she isn't,' said Morgan le Fey. 'She was quite happy to chuck you into the ovens to clean them and don't forget that the first time she did she didn't know you were fireproof. She only pretends to love you because you are so useful to her.'

'I suppose so,' said Romeo.

'You know so,' said Morgan le Fey. 'Now you are free of her.'

'But won't she come looking for me?'

'She may indeed, but she can only leave the floors below ground level on pain of death and I don't think she loves you enough for that.'

'She might.'

'I don't think so,' said Morgan le Fey. 'But tomorrow morning Lady Petaluna will put her serving wench disguise back on and go down and check.'

She did and came back to report that the Cook had woken up with a terrible headache and screamed her head off until everyone else had a terrible headache and then when she had discovered Romeo was missing she instantly swore to kill Blossom Scroggins, who she suspected had taken him away.

199

She had then cursed Romeo with the Curse of the Bagpipes and finally, to console herself, she had eaten the rest of the chocolate truffles, which had sent her back to sleep.

While she had been asleep one of the kitchen staff, who by chance was second cousin to Clynk the jailer, sent down for him and he had rolled her down the three flights of stone steps to the dungeons and locked her up in a cell with Potion the Mad Nun, so she could not do anyone, apart from Potion, any harm when she woke up.

'Fair enough,' said Romeo Crick. After all, he had seen his own family and beloved pig Geoffrey killed before his eyes. This had made him philosophical about life and realise that you should never waste time thinking about things that you could actually sort out quite satisfactorily in half a minute.[47]

'Now you follow my advice and not only will you never have to go near a kitchen again,' said Morgan le Fey, 'you will actually become a great knight.'

Of course, Romeo Crick was very taken with

---

[47] *Clever boy.*

this idea and instantly started being in love with Lady Petaluna again. If he was a great knight, she would be sure to love him back. For her part, Lady Petaluna had fallen deeply in love with Romeo Crick in the only way an eleven-year-old girl can fall in love with an eleven-year-old boy, the first moment she saw him. She had told herself that because he was just a humble kitchen minion – even though he was fireproof, which was very attractive and all that – she could never love him. Now that he was going to become a great knight, everything would be wonderful and she instantly started being in love with him again.

Morgan le Fey explained about the dragon problem and the blocked drains and told him how the Royal Messengers were scouring the Kingdom for a Brave Knight to kill the dragons and save the day.

'Though when I say save the day,' she said, 'I mean save the humans' day. Not so much the dragons'.'

'But aren't dragons an endangered species?' said Romeo.

'Thankfully, yes,' said Morgan le Fey. 'And now we must throw away your rags and attire you in clothes fit for a great knight.'

There was one thing that Romeo Crick had owned for as long as he could remember and it was the piece of string that he wore tied round his waist.

'I will need to keep my magic string,' he said, 'but I can always wear it underneath my new clothes.'

He lifted his arms and Morgan le Fey removed his rough hessian tunic, his best one with 'Finest Potatoes' written on the back.

Then she fainted.[48]

Lady Petaluna held an onion under Morgan le Fey's nose until she came round. Then the Princess looked at Romeo again and fainted some more.

'My lady,' said Lady Petaluna in a scared voice, 'what ails you?'

'His back, look.'

'He bears a strange birthmark,' said Lady Petaluna.

'You do not know what it is?'

---

[48] *Don't be disgusting, it's nothing like that and anyway, it's only his top she's taken off.*

'No.'

'It is the Mark of the King,' whispered Morgan le Fey. 'This boy is the true King of Avalon.'

'But your brother . . .' Lady Petaluna began.

'Is not my brother. Romeo is my brother,' said Morgan le Fey.

She fell to her knees and kissed Romeo's feet.

'I always knew something was wrong,' she said. 'Petaluna, go as fast as you can and bring Merlin to me.'

'Bring Merlin here?' said Lady Petaluna. 'Are you sure, my lady?'

'Of course I am sure. Everything is different now,' said Morgan le Fey. 'Absolutely everything.'

'Go to the North-West Wing?' said Merlin when Lady Petaluna found him. 'Go to the rooms of Morgan le Fey? Surely you are mistaken?'

'No, my lord,' said Lady Petaluna. 'I thought so too, but my lady insists. She says, my lord, it is more important than your dislike of each other. She says it is above all that and the whole world is changed.'

As the old wizard followed Lady Petaluna back to the North-West Wing, he suspected there was

203

only one thing it could be. He felt his heart begin to soar with happiness, but his brain told his heart to grow up and calm down. If his thoughts were right, this was the biggest thing to hit Avalon since an extremely big asteroid had landed on a remote hilltop and turned it into an extremely deep lake.

No, no, he told himself. *The King is the King and he was not swapped at birth. Oh that it were true and we are to be rid of the idiot boy who rules over us all. It cannot be. It is too much to hope for.*

But it was true.

It had always been true, the suspicion that had haunted him from the day of Arthur's birth, and here was the evidence before his own eyes.

He fell to his knees and kissed Romeo's feet.

'Your majesty,' he said. 'I always dreamt of this day, but feared it was just a wishful dream.'

Morgan le Fey reached down and touched the old man on his shoulder. They did not need to speak. That simple touch told them both that they were no longer enemies. The Dark Ages were at an end and the Nice Bright Sunny Ages were about to begin.

'Excuse me,' said Romeo Crick, who everyone

had forgotten to tell what had happened. 'Is this, like, what happens when someone gets made a great knight?'

'A great knight? My lord, you are the greatest knight of all,' said Merlin. 'You are the true King Arthur, ruler of Avalon.'

'Um, OK,' said Romeo Crick, assuming it was all some sort of practical joke.

Lady Petaluna brought a mirror so that Romeo could see the royal birthmark on his back.

'Oh,' said Romeo/Arthur. 'In the village they all told me it was the Curse of the Haddock, which I bore because I had been fished out of the river.'

'No, no, the Curse of the Haddock is completely different,' Merlin explained. 'That looks like a big crown, whereas the Mark of the King looks like this.'

'A big fish?'

'Exactly.'

The King is, um, not the King. Hooray! Long live the King.

'Let me tell him. Let me tell him,' Morgan le Fey insisted. 'I am SO going to enjoy this.'

The King Arthur who wasn't King Arthur was sitting in the middle of the floor with his back to everyone and was so absorbed playing with his toy soldiers that he didn't hear them come up behind him.

'I am the greatest King who has ever lived,' he said. 'And you are powerless against the Great Knights of Camelot, the greatest of whom, of course, is me.'

He leant forward and with a sweep of his arm sent the rows of toy soldiers flying, leaving only a small group of toy knights on horseback standing in front of him.

'Actually, you are a nasty spoilt little brat,' said Morgan le Fey. 'You are not a knight. You are not great and you are not even a king.'

As the King Arthur who wasn't King Arthur spun round, Morgan le Fey stepped forward and flattened his toy knights under her foot.

'GUARDS! GUARDS!' the boy shouted at

the top of his tiny voice, but no one came.

Merlin had told Captain of the Guard what was happening.

'NANNY! NANNY!' he shouted, but Nana Agnys did not come either.

Merlin had spoken to her too and she was having counselling for having devoted her heart and life to a fake king.

'How dare you talk to your King like that?' cried the King Arthur who wasn't King Arthur. 'You may be my sister, but I will not stand for such insubordination. I will send you to the Island of Vegetables with Mother.'

'Mother is dead because of you,' said Morgan le Fey. 'But the point is that you are not actually King Arthur.'

'Don't be stupid, of course I am.'

'No, you and the real King were swapped at birth,' said Merlin. 'I have suspected it since you first spoke. The midwife who attended your mother saw a large bird flying away just after you were born and we now know it was carrying away the baby that is the true King Arthur.'

'Don't be ridiculous. Who has put you up to this?' said King Arthur who wasn't King Arthur. 'I will have you all sent to the Island of Vegetables for this treason.'

'There is a simple test,' said Morgan le Fey. 'Take off your shirt.'

'And reveal my perfect body to you lowly commoners? Never.'

'If you don't,' said Morgan le Fey, 'I will take it off for you.'

'I don't think so,' said King Arthur who wasn't King Arthur. 'You may be a Top Royal Princess, but even you may not touch one hair of my supreme person.'

'Rot,' said Morgan le Fey and pulled the boy's shirt up over his head.

'See, there is the proof,' said Merlin. 'The boy has no Mark of the King on his back.'

'Oh well, yes, of course not,' said King Arthur who wasn't King Arthur. 'My body is a perfect sacred temple. It does not even have so much as a tiny mole to mar its unparalleled beauty.'

'Quite so,' said Merlin, 'But every single King

of Avalon since time immemorial has had the Mark of the King on his back.'

'Oh, that,' said King Arthur who wasn't King Arthur. 'The horrid crown thing. I had that removed.'

'It is not a crown,' said Morgan le Fey. 'If you were the true King you would know that.'

'Oh, yes, of course. I meant to say the other mark, the, er, um, you know.'

'Yes, we know, but you do not,' said Morgan le Fey. 'Guards, take him away. Take him down to the dungeons and put him in the cell with the Cook. I think she may have need of a new assistant.'

Word soon spread that the King Arthur who wasn't King Arthur had been replaced by a King Arthur who was the proper King Arthur and that he was not only much nicer and more intelligent than the impostor, but that his legs looked even better in mauve tights.

'Not that I actually want to wear tights, mauve or otherwise,' said the Romeo Crick who was the real King Arthur.

It was Lady Petaluna's twelfth birthday and as Romeo Crick, who henceforth will be called King

Arthur, didn't know when his birthday was, he decided it was his twelfth birthday too, and because he was King everyone agreed.

Now he was King and on the same level as Lady Petaluna, the wonderful indigestion feeling came back and he had to turn away to hide his blushes hoping that no one had noticed them.

Nobody had, apart from Morgan le Fey, Merlin, Lady Petaluna and Fremsley the Royal Whippet, who had just walked into the room to complain that he wasn't getting nearly enough attention or doggy treats.[49]

And because Romeo Crick was now King Arthur, the old pretend King Arthur needed a new name. No one knew who he really was or where he had come from.[50] It was assumed he was from a poor peasant family because if he had been someone important, there would have been an outcry when he had been stolen, whereas in the old days, peasant babies got lost all the time. Some got eaten by dragons

---

[49] *This will be remedied in* The Dragons Book 2 *when Fremsley will be revealed as a true superhero.*

[50] *Except whoever it was who had swapped the babies over in the first place.*

211

or squashed under sleeping cows. Some were carried away by giant birds to be raised as bird babies, which only worked until they tried to fly for the first time, and some really tiny babies simply blew away in the wind. The peasants just accepted it as part of life.

'Plenty more where that one came from,' they said and got on with their lives.

'We will let the Cook decide what he shall be called,' said Merlin. 'She is, after all, going to be the closest thing he's got to a family.[51] Better tell her that this one isn't fireproof, too, otherwise there'll be no point in giving him a name.'

To say the ex-King was angry was like saying crocodiles are cuddly. When the Cook was let out of the cell and stuck the boy under her arm to carry him back up to the kitchen, he kicked and screamed so much that the hairs in her armpit caught fire.

'I can see we're going to have to make some changes here,' said the Cook.

'Don't talk to me like that, you big, fat ugly stupid peasant,' the ex-King screamed.

'Quite a lot of changes, I reckons,' she said.

---

[51] *Which was about as close as penguins are to the North Pole.*

'Put me down this minute or I'll have you thrown in jail and tortured and poked with pointy sticks!' he yelled.

The Cook reached up and took a large wire basket down from a hook in the kitchen ceiling. It was where she kept the hens' eggs and was just the right size to keep a small ex-King safely locked up. He smashed the seven eggs in the basket, which did no one any harm except himself.

'I need a bath,' he cried. 'Fetch Nana Agnys.'

'A bath?' said the Cook. 'The likes of you don't have baths.'

'Well, I'm sticky,' the boy demanded. 'I need a bath. NOW!'

So the Cook threw a bucket of cold water over him. The water poured down onto the range below and as it hit the hot metal it turned into a great cloud of steam.

'There, your majesty,' laughed the Cook, 'not just a bath but a sauna too.'

Then she summoned all the kitchen hands and asked them to suggest a name for the boy. Brat was very popular. In fact, everyone liked it, except for

213

Dierdre the Sink Plug Washer, who had taken a shine to the ex-King and wanted to call him Mine.

'OK, Brat it is,' said the Cook.

So Brat sat in his wire cage glaring down at everyone and vowed that one day, he would have his revenge. From the Cook right up to the King, he would get them all.

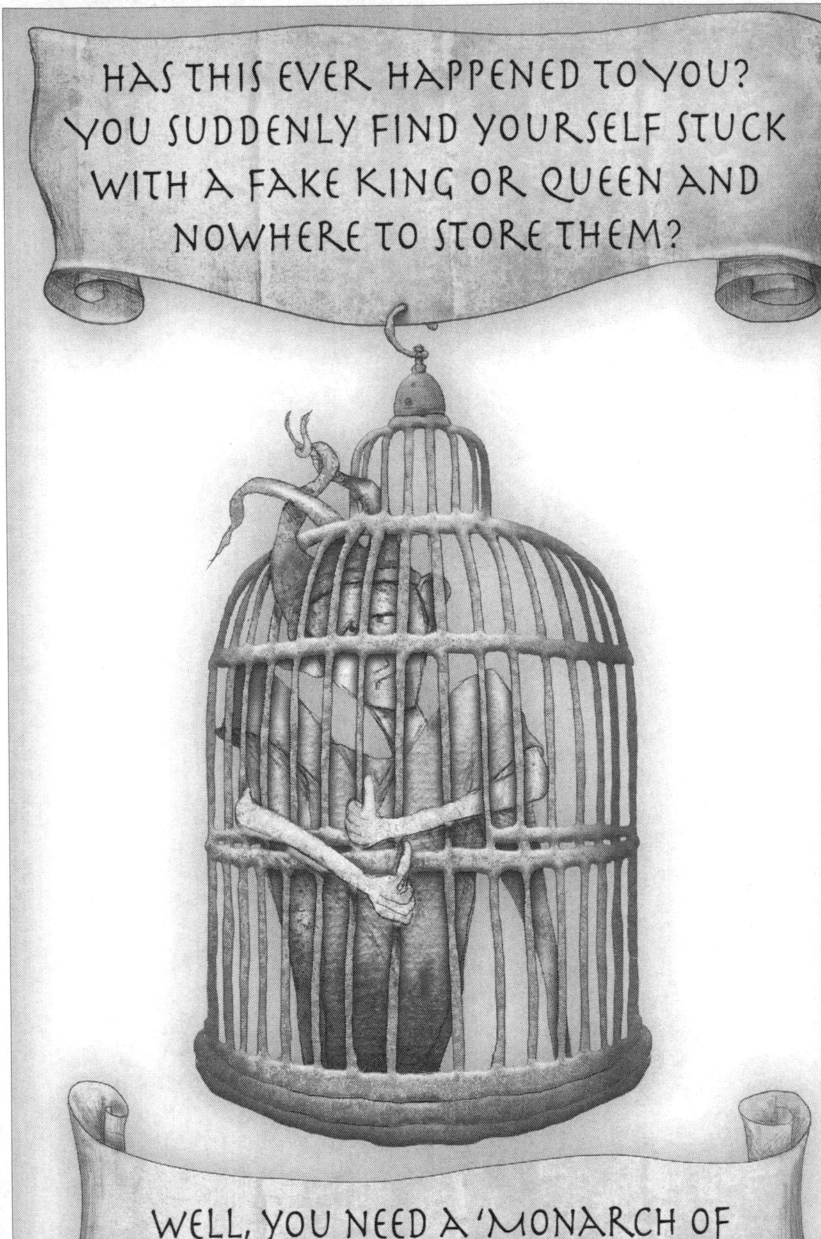

ADVERTISEMENT

Finally, eventually, at last and in conclusion.

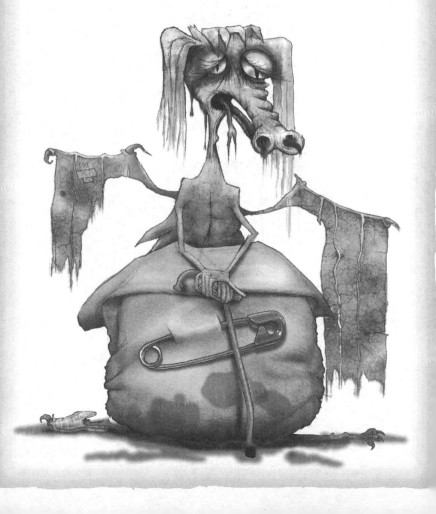

'Obviously, the first thing we must do is fix the drains,' said King Arthur.

'Indeed, sire,' said Merlin, who did not know the boy's unique talent, 'but the only way in is through the secret tunnel at the back of the dragon's cave. It would be certain death for anyone who enters.'

'Oh yes,' said Morgan le Fey, 'in all the excitement, I forgot to tell you. There is someone who can reach the tunnel unharmed.'

'You mean the four Royal Messengers have returned with a Brave Knight?'

'No. The person I'm talking about is right here among us.'

'But who?'

'Our own King, my newly discovered beloved little brother, Arthur.'

'My lady!' said Merlin in horror. 'You would send our great King to his death?'

'What she means,' said King Arthur, 'is that I am fireproof. When I was five years old, the dragons came to our village and burnt it to the ground. I alone

217

survived. Well, apart from my best friend, Geoffrey, but he was stuck by lightning soon after . . .' Arthur stopped speaking and stared dreamily into space.

'Your majesty?'

'Sorry, I was just remembering how delicious Geoffrey tasted,' said King Arthur. The others looked horrified and he hastily explained that Geoffrey had been a pig. 'I survived because I was fireproof.'

'It's true,' said Morgan le Fey. 'The Cook used to send him into the red-hot ovens to clean them out and not a single hair on his head was touched.'

'But the dragons don't just breathe fire,' said Merlin. 'They've got great big sharp teeth. I doubt our King is biteproof.'

'Ah, yes,' said everyone.

'We need a distraction,' said Arthur. 'A Brave Knight to lure the dragons out of their cave, while I slip past into the tunnel.'

'Unfortunately none of the Royal Messengers have returned with one,' said Merlin.

But then the door flew open and a mighty figure strode into the room.

'That is not quite true,' said the mighty figure, bowing low before the King and even lower before Morgan le Fey, who blushed bright red. 'I am Sir Lancelot of Croydon and I am at your majesty's and at your lady's service.'

'Really?' said Morgan le Fey.

'Indeed, my lady,' said Sir Lancelot. 'I would be your Champion.'

'Champion what?' said Morgan le Fey.

'No, no, my lady. Your Champion,' said Sir Lancelot. 'It means I would serve you and fight your fights and guard your honour, my lady, until the last breath in my body.'

'Sounds good,' said Morgan le Fey. 'OK, you can be my Champion.'

'But first, good knight,' the King began.

'Good night?' said Merlin. 'It's not bed-time yet, is it?'[52]

'But first,' the King continued, 'we need you to slay the dragon.'

'No, no, dear brother,' said Morgan le Fey. 'Not actually slay it. After all, they are an endangered

---

[52] *Hey, I love puns and the best puns are the worst puns.*

219

species so I don't think we should actually make them extinct. What we need Sir Lancelot to do is just distract them while you nip into the cave.'

'Fair enough,' said King Arthur. 'So not so much charging at them with your sword, more like poking your tongue out at them and calling them rude names and running away a bit with them chasing you, and . . . Could you say that first bit again?'

'First bit?' said Morgan le Fey.

'Yes, the "dear brother" bit,' said Arthur. 'I've never been a brother before.'

'Well, my dear brother, you have actually been a dear brother since you were born,' said Morgan le Fey. 'You just didn't know it.'

'My lady,' said Sir Lancelot, bowing before Morgan le Fey. 'Your will is my command. We shall set out at dawn.'

'Are you sure you don't want him to slay the dragons, even a little bit?' said Merlin, who was very much into the old ways.

'No,' said the King. 'No blood is to be spilt.'

220

'Uh oh,' said Primrose the next morning. 'Humans coming.'

She had seen the party of humans crossing the bridges and islands, and now they were approaching the Valley of the Dragons.

'I bet they've got their thumbs with them, haven't they?' said Spikeweed, King of the Dragons.

'Well, of course they have. They're humans. Now get out there and do battle.'

'Do I have to?' said Spikeweed. 'I've got a dreadful cold and you've no idea how disgusting that is when you start breathing fire, great gobs of snot everywhere. I mean . . .'

'Too much information,' said Primrose. 'So go out there and sneeze at them.'

It was traditional when humans and dragons came into contact with each other that a human messenger was sent out to negotiate.

The negotiation usually went something like this:

Dragon: *What do you want?*

Human: *We come in peace.*

Dragon: *No you don't.*

Human: *Yes we do, honest.*

Dragon: *Go away.*

Human: *But we'd really like to come and live in this beautiful place.*

Dragon: *Well, of course you would. Who wouldn't?*

Human: *So, can we?*

Dragon: *No. Sod off.*

Human: *You'll be hearing from our solicitors.*

Dragon, shooting out flames and toasting the messenger: *And you'll be hearing from my nose.*

The end result was usually a few toasted messengers followed by another population of dragons wiped out by angry humans.

This time it had been decided to take a different approach. The humans didn't want to kill any dragons, but they didn't want the dragons to know that. So Sir Lancelot rode up on his big horse and ————— them.

222

'Oi, stupid lizards,' he cried out, 'I would come and talk to you but you are so stinky I can't bear to come any nearer.'

Spikeweed was torn. The one thing dragons hate more than anything, apart from not having thumbs, is being called lizards. On the other hand, the smell from his old incontinent granny, Gorella, was super-double stinky. He couldn't argue with that.

'Did you hear me, lizardy lizard-face?' Sir Lancelot shouted. 'You great big ugly thumbless lump.'

'Thumbless? Thumbless? That does it,' roared Spikeweed and raced out of the cave followed by Primrose, the two eldest kids and a lot of baby dragons that kept getting under their feet and tripping them up. The babies hadn't the faintest idea what was going on, but it was all very exciting and they ran around all over the place biting each other and crashing into rocks.

As the dragons chased Sir Lancelot up the valley, King Arthur slipped into the cave and ran towards the entrance to the secret tunnel.

'Oh no,' he cried when he got there.

The ancient, seriously stinky Gorella was lying right across the entrance with a whole lot more baby dragons climbing all over her. She was fast asleep on her back, snoring and leaking horribly.

There was nothing for it. Holding his breath, King Arthur climbed over the old dragon and into the tunnel. His eyes were watering and he felt very, very sick. But actually, the smell of Gorella made the smell of the blocked sewers seem almost pleasant by comparison.

Being babies, the young dragons hadn't learnt that humans were supposed to be their enemies so they ran after him.

Arthur pushed the explosives he had brought with him into gaps in the pile of rocks. This took a lot longer than he had hoped because the baby dragons thought it was a game and kept pulling the explosive sticks out of the rocks and bringing them back to him. Finally he managed to bury them under rocks that were too big to move and walked back down the tunnel, trailing the fuse behind him. He then knelt down to light the fuse, but the dragons' cave was so damp it wouldn't light.

Behind him, he could hear a commotion. The dragons had got fed up chasing Sir Lancelot and come back.

'Oops,' said Arthur.

'What have we here?' said Spikeweed.

'I'll tell you what,' said Arthur. 'What we have here is a situation.'

'Oh really?' said Spikeweed. 'I don't see a situation. I see lunch. Though I must admit it will be difficult to make someone as small and weedy as you feed the whole family.'

'I'm not your lunch,' said Arthur.

'I must say, little human, you are remarkably calm for someone who is about to get lightly barbecued on both sides and eaten,' said Spikeweed.

'Yes, because it's not going to happen,' said Arthur. He held out his hand. 'Have a go.'

Primrose snorted out a white-hot flame, which, of course, had absolutely no effect on Arthur.

'I am Arthur, King of Avalon,' said King Arthur, 'and I am fireproof.'

'Well, I am Spikeweed, King of the Dragons,' Spikeweed said, 'and I make fire.'

'Pleased to meet you,' said Arthur.

'Roarin' brave, aren't you?' said Spikeweed.

'Well, if you were to harm me, the great wizard Merlin would bring every single human down on you and make your entire species extinct and not just you, but your fancy Italian relatives too,' said Arthur. 'On the other hand, if we become allies just think what we could do together.'

'That makes sense,' said Primrose.

'But I am Spikeweed, King of the Dragons. I am powerful and ferocious,' said Spikeweed. 'I am genetically programmed to hate humans.'

'Oh, grow up, you stupid twit,' said Primrose.

'She's right, Dad,' said Bloat and Depressyng.

'Oh, all right,' said Spikeweed. 'I, Spikeweed, King of The Dragons, hereby form an alliance with you, Arthur, King of Avalon.'

'And to seal our treaty,' said Arthur, 'we will do each other one deed of kindness.'

'Fair enough,' said Spikeweed. 'What?'

'See that fuse in the tunnel there? Well, could one of you set it alight?'

'No problem,' said Spikeweed.

226

'And in return, my servants shall bring you incontinence pants and lots and lots of bars of soap for your old granny.'

'Incontinence pants,' said Primrose with a tear in her eye. 'That's the nicest thing anyone's ever done for us.'

As King Arthur was being given a hero's welcome outside the cave for bringing peace between humans and dragons, the ground shook and suddenly every bath and every lavatory in Camelot was free.

The blast also blew all the doors off the prison cells and the thirteen prisoners were free too.

Including Lord Resydue the Baby-Eater of Londinium . . .

Postscript 1
Living happily ever after

Later that evening, King Arthur and Morgan le Fey sat at the top of the tallest tower in Camelot and watched the sun set over the moat.

'You know,' said Arthur. 'It doesn't really get much better than this.'

Oh yes it does, thought Morgan le Fey. *A lot better.*

But she said nothing.

Postscript 2
Living happily ever after

Later that evening, King Spikeweed, Primrose and their fifty-two children sat at the top of the tall mountain and watched the sun set over their valley.

'You know,' said Spikeweed. 'It doesn't really get much better than this.'

Oh yes it does, thought Primrose. *The kids will all grow up and leave home.*

But she said nothing.

 ost-postscript

If you are wondering about Fremsley the Royal Whippet, and I know I am, I'm afraid we've run out of space. BUT worry not for Fremsley will appear in *The Dragons Book 2*, in which he will perform incredible feats of great endurance like sleeping all day under some really heavy blankets, pausing only to eat his dinner before settling down for a good night's sleep.

230

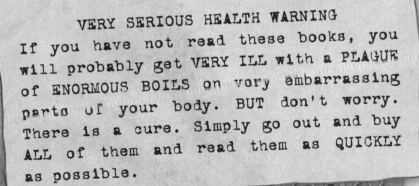

THE **FLOODS**
NEIGHBOURS

THE **FLOODS**
PLAYSCHOOL

VERY SERIOUS HEALTH WARNING
If you have not read these books, you
will probably get VERY ILL with a PLAGUE
of ENORMOUS BOILS on very embarrassing
parts of your body. BUT don't worry.
There is a cure. Simply go out and buy
ALL of them and read them as QUICKLY
as possible.

PRIME SUSPECT

WANTED

THE FLOODS
GANG

F.S.I.

Colin Thompson

THE GREAT OUTDOORS

Colin Thompson

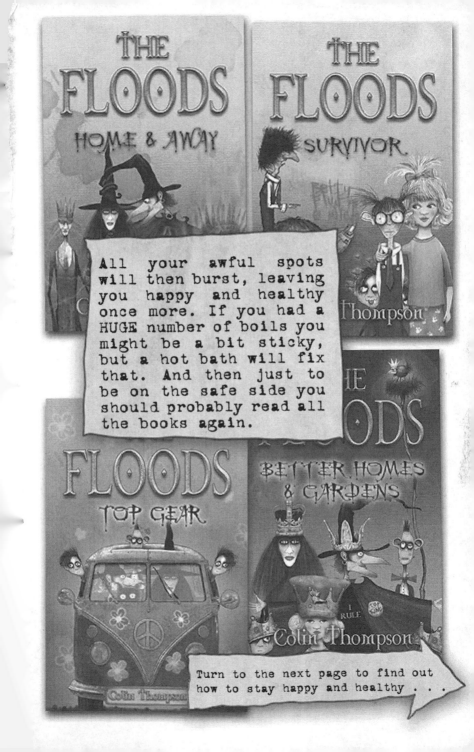

THE **FLOODS**
HOME & AWAY

THE **FLOODS**
SURVIVOR

Thompson

All your awful spots will then burst, leaving you happy and healthy once more. If you had a HUGE number of boils you might be a bit sticky, but a hot bath will fix that. And then just to be on the safe side you should probably read all the books again.

FLOODS
TOP GEAR

Colin Thompson

...E
...ODS

BETTER HOMES & GARDENS

I RULE

Colin Thompson

Turn to the next page to find out how to stay happy and healthy . . .

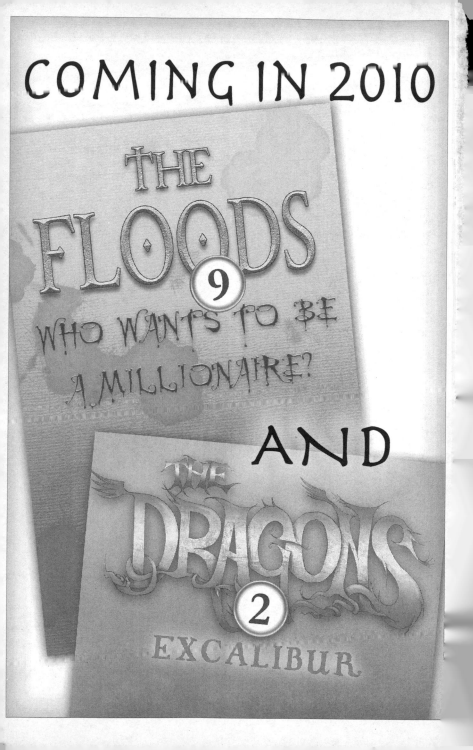